Rebound 1977

S H A D O W E D !

Sleuth E (with an accent), being Hippolyte, French Secret Agent, whom no one could take for anything but an Englishman

Frontispiece]

SHADOWED!

By

Hilaire Belloc

with

Thirty-seven Drawings by

G. K. Chesterton

Harper & Brothers, Publishers

New York and London

1929

LIST OF ILLUSTRATIONS

5557

LIST OF ILLUSTRATIONS

S H A D O W E D !

CHAP 1

You may well call him Chap 1 ; for he is the first Chap I am going to talk about. Have no fear. He will not detain you long.

He was walking briskly down Fifth Avenue in the City of New York on a rather too hot June day of the year 1979. He was a man of something over thirty, short, and broad-shouldered ; with a new straw hat on his queer head, and a light grey suit off the hook. In his right hand he swung a small new and smart attaché case, bearing the letters L. Z. A close observer would have seen that on the corner of his handkerchief which just showed from his pocket were the letters D. M.—in red silk. But then I am not a close observer, and neither are you ; so we will not dwell too much on that. A really curious enquirer, who should have waited till he swung his hat, would have seen in the crown of it, tastefully embossed, the gilt letters J. F.

7

He had very pale green eyes, somewhat turtive though decided, too wide apart, and with a Mongolian lift at the outer corners : high cheek bones, a round face, and a skin which might be called a dirty yellow or a delicate parchment, according to whether one were engaged in flattering him or no. His rather scanty straight hair, a little too long at the back, projected from the hat above recorded. He was clean-shaven. His left cheek carried the pronounced scar of a sabre-cut, now nearly ten years old.

So walked he smartly down town by way of Fifth Avenue.

He was just about to turn into Tenth Street, and he was already within two blocks of the Travel Agency for which he was making, to take up his steamer reservation for England, when a tall man, in a slouch hat, coming suddenly upon him from the side street, touched his ·arm and stopped him in his stride. Even as he thus abruptly halted, a lanky, inane-looking man, wearing a look of indifference and innocence which would have made him suspected in the most crass company, stopped as abruptly, struck by something in a shop window. He was about fifty yards behind the pair who had thus met, and that was natural enough as he was paid to follow the man with the scar and had been keeping at that distance ever since Chap I had stepped out of his hotel nearly a mile back.

The scarred man and his tall, slouch-hatted friend turned down into Tenth Street at a leisurely pace, talking together : and the lanky gentlemanly man, at his due distance, did the same. But he now moved rather more quickly ; he caught the pair up, passed them hastily, got just before them into the Travel Agency, and asked to look at the folder of the Dutch Line.

The two came in just as he buried his face in that piece of literature, and he heard the scarred one speak to the clerk at the counter.

" You know that reservation of mine on the *Zeeland*," he said. " Number 136 ? The single cabin on the top deck ? Port side ? "

He spoke clearly and quickly, with no very recognisable accent, and yet it was not exactly English. It would have puzzled anyone to say what it was, but it certainly was not peculiar to any district of the United States, still less of England.

Even as he spoke the man in the slouch hat muttered in another tongue, " Not so loud ! We are observed ! " But it was too late, the number had passed.

" Number 136 ? " said the clerk. " Yes ? "

" Not so loud ! We are observed ! "

And even as he said it, the lanky, inane-looking man, who had been searching in the Dutch Line folder, handed it back. He had heard all he wanted to hear : and it was as well not to stay too long. Perhaps these gentlemen were used to recognising research workers of his kind. He went out sauntering like a man with no particular business before him and a fine incapacity for it if he had.

As for the other two, the slouch-hatted one added not a word, and the scarred one said no more than that he was giving up the cabin ; he could not travel by that boat. The clerk told him the ticket was made out—which it wasn't—and must be paid for : a large sum, for the man with the scar looked after himself well. But he made no protest. He did not even ask to see the ticket. He had the money ready in his hand in notes, which he had pulled loose from his pocket. He did not delay to ask if he might get a refund if they should manage to fill the berth before the boat sailed, nor to make any of those objections which men usually make when they have to forfeit money uselessly. His gesture was that of one who knew exactly what he would have to give and was prepared to give it ; of one, moreover, to whom the sum forfeited was of no consequence.

He took the receipt, signed the form acknowledging the giving up of his berth, and went out with his companion. The scarred man hailed a taxi, and as they both got in he gave the address of his hotel.

· Meanwhile the lanky, vacuous-looking person was at the telephone. He was already in a public box. Before Chap 1 and slouch-hat were well round the corner, he had already rung up the Plantagenet Club and asked for the General Manager of the Truth and Justice Private Enquiry Company, commonly known as the T. and J.

That Great Personage, the trusted ally of Mighty Governments and still more mighty Banks—let alone Monopolists, Share Shufflers, and other individual powers—came quickly to his end of the wire. For he was eager and anxious. The Distributing Centre in France had cabled three times in one day, so urgent was it, and he hadn't yet got the berth or the boat, let alone the names under which Chap 1 was concealing his very interesting personality.

Very welcome therefore in the ears of the Manager of the T. and J. was his employe's voice.

" That the T. and J. ? Mister Harrison ? . . . Good. The *Zeeland*—136," he said . . . " Nope. Never mind the name. I'll get that later. I know that sort. I wasn't going to let him take my

portrait. Yes, I know she sails to-night. I'm
going right around now to the quay. I'll get his
name on the list and ring you up again then. And
I'll sure shoot him, too. You set right there. I'll
ring again at a quarter of the hour . . ."

At the other end of the wire the Superintendent
stepped out of the telephone box in his club, and
told the servant to send for him the moment they
rang him up again. He pulled out his watch.

" It'll be at a quarter of the hour," he said. And
he muttered : " Time enough too ! He's only got
to step round to the Dutch Line wharf."

There was some disappointment in his face, which
was remarkable for exactly resembling the face of
any other great Business Brain : being, as it were, of
wood, also set, strawng and tortoiseshell-spectacled.
He mused in anxiety.

He had to trust Evans (John). An experienced
man. Same man as had gotten Sadie James her
Ali-mony by that scoop with the Gimlet at the
Merron House. What he said, went. Mebbe it *was*
unwise to linger in that Travel Agency, but the
Manager of the T. and J. couldn't help thinking
that Evans (John) might at least have glanced
without danger at the name on the Reservation.
However, 'tweren't long to wait.

He sat in tension and attempted to allay the torture of suspense by recalling his success—such as it was—up to that point.

The Distributing Centre in France had cabled in code forty-eight hours before, that Z. (it was the only name they gave him) was in New York, to their certain knowledge ; they must have his movements—probably for England. He had found his man at the Belton, signed on as Malder. He had spotted the name his quarry had gone under after slipping past the frontier from British Columbia. It was Davis. He knew, too, that on the books of the Paramount Hotel in Chicago it had been Hackenschmidt. Both very good names, but not much alike. That was good work for less than two days—and had cost—oh ! Hell. Now, at the Belton it was Malder. He was certain that for the trip to Europe it would be a fourth name, quite different from either of the other three. It was essential that he should get it. They'd cabled three times again. It would lower his stock badly if he failed : he didn't want to have to cable with only the berth and no name ; the folk at the European end wouldn't be cold sure on a number without a name to confirm it . . . However, that's all there was to it. It would be fixed in five minutes more. He looked at his watch. He had only to wait that minute and he'd know. Anyhow, he couldn't cable till they'd seen the liner start and him aboard it, sure.

The quarter of the hour came . . . and passed . . . and ten minutes. The hour struck by the fine old Colonial grandfather clock, which was the pride of the Club, and being younger than the Porter, kept better time. The head of the Great T. and J. Agency began to sweat. He jerked out into the hall, asked them if they were certain no one had rung up ; he jerked back again to the rooms, picked up an evening paper, couldn't read it, threw it down again, jerked back again to the hall. The quarter past struck, and yet there was no message. He waited till the half hour, and by that time he was in a panic. There was not much more than an hour left before the *Zeeland* would sail.

The delay was due to such a simple thing ! The lanky, inane-faced one had rightly determined that it was quicker to walk from the Travel Agency to the North River than to hire, seeing what traffic conditions were. On this account it was that he had been knocked down by a charming little car driven by a charming little woman, just as he was crossing Sixth Avenue. He was fortunate in the

*Tortures of Suspense suffered in the Plantagenet
Club of New York by the Manager of the
Truth and Justice Enquiry Corporation*

manner of his death. He never knew what struck him. It was quick work.

Far off North in the Plantagenet Club the President of the Great T. and J. Agency was thinking intensely and rapidly. If he went down himself to the boats, he might miss a belated message. If he stayed where he was, he might have to wait indefinitely. Something had gone wrong. He decided on a second string. It was against his general policy ; he never liked more than one man to know about one job. But it was urgent. There was not an hour before the *Zeeland* sailed.

He rang up the office and asked for Merriman. When he got Merriman he gave him very precise instructions. That worthy was to go down to the Dutch Line, end of 17th, and find who had booked berth 136, port side, top deck, on the *Zeeland*, sailing that evening at 6. He might suit himself as to how he got the name, but he must get it ; there was no difficulty there ; he could look up the list. They'd have it printed by this time. All that was to be done at once. Then he was to go and get a squint of the guy, and note all details ; and if he could shoot him and get a picture, why, it would be double fee. Then he was to make sure that the boat had sailed with the guy on

2

board, and come up town and ask for him at the
Plantagenet Club. The Manager would wait there
for him.

There, that was all over.

Meanwhile, in the taxi, the man with the scar and
the man with the slouch hat were talking in a language
which neither you nor I would have understood, but
which had been theirs from the cradle ; and most of
the talking was done by the man with the slouch
hat, and most of the listening by the man with the
scar.

There was not much to say or to listen to. It was
not ten minutes from the place where they had
hailed the cab to the hotel. But in the interval the
man with the slouch hat had given the man with
the scar the very simple information that he had
been spotted as Davis, spotted as Hackenschmidt,
traced to the taking of his Reservation, and that
that was why he had given that sharp order for the
berth to be given up. The next step had been
thought out ; of course. An alternative berth had
been taken. When they got to the hotel he would
give him his travelling name. The number of
the berth was 97, the boat was an old one of the
Swedish line, the *Bergen*. He could go aboard
that night. That didn't matter. There was no

hurry. She touched first at Plymouth, he could land there.

*   *   *   *

I am sorry that the world should be so full of men, but here is another man coming on the stage. A pleasing, good, and simple man, quite young— barely twenty-six—one whom it would be an insult to call a barber's block, but too much of a compliment to call an Adonis ; reasonably tall, more than reasonably well-made, slim, healthy as one is at that age, with a moustache of the old fashion, smooth, brown, sufficient and not exaggerated, and hair exactly matched. An easy gait after the English model, and a silver-head cane, carried rather consciously, as though to say, " Oh ! yes ! call me English if you like ! I'm proud of it ! " Indeed, an expert would have sworn to his name as Algernon. But no, it was not even Percy. It was Richard—Richard Mallard—and English as the names were, he that bore them had never seen England.

As this pleasing sight came into the Travel Bureau, a quarter of an hour after the battle-scarred one and his sinister colleague had left it, the only point in which you would have distinguished him out of a crowd of other good-looking young men, at least before he began to speak, was an expression of simplicity and timidity in his soft brown eyes, and the betrayal in his gestures of a certain nervousness and haste. When he spoke, his English also had that touch of a something foreign—one could hardly tell what—in the accent ; but it was not an echo of the battle-scarred one's accent, it was different, it was from another clime, as indeed was the young man altogether, for you could see that by blood he was in part of English lineage.

He had a very simple question to ask, and an apparently equally simple motive, and made no effort to conceal them. He was in a hurry for that berth to Europe. Was there a boat starting that very evening ? Was there any chance of going aboard ? It was rush time, he knew, but perhaps there was a cancelled berth ? It was a point-blank method, possible only since the repeal of the Farman regulations, and it succeeded. I am glad it succeeded, for the young man clearly wanted to get away.

" Oh ! I say," he began, as he stood humbly enough at the counter, " I wonder if you happen to have a berth—what ? "

The clerk went through that ritual which commercial morals demand — saying that it was

" I say—what ?"

absolutely impossible, then bethinking him of the possibility ; then setting the wires to work, with some of the telephone messages genuine enough, and the others sham ; making a great favour of the whole affair, pocketing a corresponding premium, and finally making out a ticket for the cancelled berth ; and the name on the ticket was Richard Mallard.

How often it happens in this world that everyone is pleased, and that no harm is done ! It sounds impossible, for it sounds like perpetual motion ; but it is always happening. There was this nice young gentleman going out of the Travel Bureau, having got his berth at the last moment by the most exceptional luck—for which he did not mind paying ; there was the clerk, with something like a fortnight's salary in his pocket ; and there was the Shipping Company, with an extra five hundred and thirty-five dollars over and above the capacity of the *Zeeland*, which five hundred and thirty-five dollars would spread themselves in various amounts over some two thousand shareholders, but with the greater part ultimately payable to a paralytic upon the Riviera ; and there was the Mysterious Stranger, who had sacrificed his berth, saved from the jaws of destruction. So far as I can figure it out, the only person who suffered for a moment in the whole business was the tall, gentlemanly, vacuous man, who was run over by the pretty little woman in her car in the middle of Sixth Avenue ; and after all, he exchanged this world for a better, and, as I have been careful to tell you, his death was swift and painless. Not even the Boss of the Big Enquiry Company was for long disturbed. For he got all the information he wanted, as you shall shortly hear, and slept that night a contented man.

*   *   *   *

Mr. Merriman, that faithful, alert and joyous slave of duty, was sleuthing Berth Number 136.

When Richard Mallard (please to remember that it was his *real* name, for there may be a good deal of mix 'em and gather 'em about this book) came striding up the gangway, registering Simplicity and Relief and a sufficient dose of timidity—what ? his first remark on hitting the deck with his right foot was to call out the number of his cabin to the first official he saw, for the sake of directions. And the awaiting Merriman, praising Heaven for the astonishing earliness of his good luck, was equally direct. He slapped Richard Mallard fraternally upon the shoulder, and said : " Say, Bud, you're the man I gotta speak to ! "

It amused him not a little to observe the addressee jump perceptibly, like a man who hears a sudden shot. For Richard Mallard turned not only round but pale. His face turned round quicker than his body· (it is always a bad sign !) and both in a sort of jump. He clutched Mr. Merriman's arm, while there passed through his eyes in lightning succession the emotions of terror, bewilderment, and resignation. For Richard Mallard had suffered great agony from interviewers lately, and indeed this was the reason of his hasty flight.

" Eh ? I say—what ? " he gasped. " What do you want with me, eh ? " And even as he said it, he looked round for avenues of escape. Then he added in a lower tone, taking the private detective's arm and leading him aside, " Look here, you know, it's no good you making a row here, in public—what ? "

They were in the comparative privacy of an interval between two boats opposite the saloon door on the off side from the quay, and in the comparative silence of a donkey engine which was rattling in a chain, two hooting tugs, the first warning bell, and a quantity of steam escaping from a hellish pipe along the after funnel.

" Look here, I say, what do you want with me ? "
repeated the Emigrant to Europe.

Merriman nodded cheerfully.

" You stand right there ! " he said.

He stepped back two paces and pulled out a
camera.   He was about to shoot.

" I say ! None of that ! " shouted the unfortunate
youth as he sprang forward.   His tormentor
danced backward in glee, shouted affectionately,
" Smile ! Baby ! " clicked the little trigger, and
put the Kodak back in his pocket.   Then he
winked, like the cheerful soul he was, and stood
at ease.

" Don't do that ! " cried Richard Mallard, somewhat too late.

Merriman answered by another wink and a cheerful
nod.

" It's only for the paper, Mr. Mallard.   You won't
mind ? "

A new set of emotions chased themselves through
Richard Mallard's thumping heart.   Violence, re-
newed terror, an instinct for flight : then again for
grappling.   But his guardian angel was looking after
the really blameless young man, for he ended up
by choosing with discretion, and nourished that
most salutary spirit long enough to speak in a

" Smile ! Baby ! "

quieter tone: that is, to shout with less vehemence above the various cheerful sounds of departure.

"I don't know why you shouldn't snap me. And I don't see why you shouldn't know my name—what? If it comes to that, I could have told you where you could have bought a photograph of me, if you'd asked me decently."

"No time," said the cheerful Merriman, wagging his head.

"Why did you do it?" asked the other, his anger rising again.

Merriman sighed. "It's for me paper," he said. "They said to me, just you get down and snap any dude off for Europe, 'caws we've got to get some guy for that column called 'Birds of Passage.' You're one bird. Aw! Don't foam! I got a dozen others before you come aboard. You're just a figure, you see, for the column," he added apologetically.

"Mr. ——, I beg your pardon, what is your name?" said Mr. Mallard, trying to lower his voice, but conquered by the donkey engine.

"Timson," said Mr. Merriman at once. He had eight names ready, but lacking the capacity to use them in any system, he produced whichever came up first.

"Well, Mr. Timson," went on Richard earnestly,

" I've got something to say to you about that snap."

He stepped forward a pace, and Merriman as promptly stepped back one, remarking that monkey business was cut right out.

" It's only something I have to beg of you, and . . . and . . . I think I can make it worth your while, Mr. Timson . . .. you say you've got plenty of others ? "

Merriman nodded. But as he did so, Richard Mallard could not help observing that he fixed him with a steady glance, as if he were taking in every detail of his face and habit.

" Mr. Timson, do you know how much it's worth to me that that picture should not come out in your paper ?   By the way, what's the name of the paper ?"

" *North Pole Gazette*," answered Mr. Merriman simply.   Nor did Richard Mallard smile.

" Well, no doubt it's a syndicate," he went on hurriedly.   " But look here, they'll be ringing the second bell in a minute.   Now, I say, for God's sake do listen to me.   Eh ? what ?   Do you know what it's worth to me that that shouldn't come out in the papers ? "

" I do nawt," answered Merriman—which was the

easier, as there was no question of its coming out in any paper at all.

" It's worth one hundred dollars," affirmed the other with an odd little note of triumph in his face—as who should say, " You see ! I can pay what I like ! "

Mr. Merriman thought rapidly, as is the fashion of his kind. It is a common talent with unintelligent men.

If he stopped to bargain, the second bell might ring at any moment. On the other hand, if he bargained, who knows what the quarry might be good for ? His Chief had told him nothing of the case ; he only had the simple orders : " Find out the name attached to Berth 136 on the *Zeeland*, and make certain what the man is like." And his Chief was not in the habit of making confidants of his subordinates. Now supposing this was a character whom " they " were " waiting for " on the other side ? 136 was a swell nest and no mistake ; only one berth and right on the promenade. Or supposing it was blackmail ?

He was on the point of using that great phrase, so familiar to the captains of industry, " Nothing doing ! " when the first stroke of the second bell was heard ; and long before its clanging had filled the ship he had swivelled over to the other phrase, equally familiar to the masters of the modern world : " Done with *you !* Oh ! Boy ! " And he frankly held out his hand, not in friendship, but to receive the goods.

A huge roll came out from the inner pocket of Mr. Mallard's excellent light coat : and twenty V's from its inwards were furtively, rapidly, slipped into the detective's hand.

" Now you'll keep your word, won't you ? " said the payer, with unfailing futility.

" Yep," nodded the payee. He waved cheerfully, turned, and was gone. And Richard Mallard was left on board, a prey to the most horrid tortures of doubt.

It was essential that that picture should not appear. It was essential that his name should not be noised abroad. On the other hand, what reason had anyone to noise it abroad ? He had always read in crook stories that people to whom it was essential that their names should not be noised abroad used another name. He remembered too late this habit of the anti-noising-abroad brigade. He cursed himself for having blurted out his name so childishly when he had asked for the chance of an empty berth. Why hadn't he called himself De Vere ?

But yet again, why should his name be noised abroad ? Who knew of it up there in New York ; or anywhere, for that matter, except the place where he came from ? It was quite a private affair. No doubt the stranger had told a true story, and all they wanted was pictures for their silly column, " Birds of Passage ! "

But the picture ! The picture ! That was the rub. Nobody might care about him in New York ; but the New York Sunday papers go a long way. My God ! If they saw that picture down in travelling kit and on the steamboat deck, and that date to it ! . . . But he was getting exhausted with all this worry. It was no good borrowing trouble. He tried to convince himself that the gentleman with the camera had told a true and simple tale, and that his motive had been no more than what he had said. He tried to convince himself that Shooter had enough honesty to act by his bribe.

And so once again within a single hour all the world was satisfied (I repeat, that sort of thing is perpetually happening). Richard Mallard had run through the whole store of his anxieties and was reposing in the repose of exhaustion. Mr. Merriman had earned, over and above his salary, the prodigious sum of one hundred dollars, and double pay for

leaving at his Chief's club, within the hour, after a
short deal, the Kodak film, the name attached, to
Cabin 136, " Richard Mallard," and a good little
précis in pencil of what that person looked like,
what were his tricks of conversation, the colour of
his hair and his eyes, his moustache, his particular
gestures, and all the rest. His Boss was mightily
relieved as well : cabled to the Distributing Centre,
ordered himself a most excellent dinner, and went
home to sleep, a contented man. Even the people
on board the *Zeeland* were happy, because the night
was as calm as oil and because as they slipped
through the narrows they could drink wine freely
after the fashion of an older and a wiser world.
All were happy and no one a victim. I can't see
how it works out, but so it was.

CHAPTER II

As the *Zeeland* pushed eastward across the calm Atlantic, Richard Mallard reviewed his position; and his position was this. He was getting away at top speed to a quiet life, at last. He had known quieter. Indeed, because it was too quiet he had left it. But a very few intervening days since his leaving home had driven out of him all need for excitement.

He had already sighed profoundly with a new content two separate times since getting his dinner into him and settling down in his deck chair on that warm June night. He watched the light of Sandy Hook twinkling farther and farther away towards the summer horizon.

He had had enough of it. He was fed up to the molars. And what he had had enough of was publicity.

Richard Mallard and his place in life were the result of many manias which had haunted a certain William Mallard, retired English tobacco merchant, of a lonely, well-appointed house, El Rectoret, some twenty miles from Havana. William Mallard had been born in the later years of the 20th century and quietly died at El Rectoret in 1955. His manias had been these.

First, the mania of adopting in extreme old age a baby surreptitiously brought in from no one knew where. Some said it was the illegitimate child of his daughter, a theory which accounted for everything, and satisfied the malice of all; but with this flaw in it, that old William Mallard never had had a daughter that anyone had known or heard of; nor, for that matter, any other relative. Some said that he had adopted the baby in order to annoy those who were expecting the legacy of his small fortune. But there again, there was the crab that no one was expecting the legacy of his small fortune; though it is the fact that when he died, before this Child from Nowhere was two years old, he had left it all he had; and that was a great deal less than most people had expected.

His will was ample proof of a further mania. The boy was left under the guardianship of American lawyers in the island, with a mass of detailed provisions all bound down strictly in law. Little Richard " seeing that he was of English descent "

(there was no other proof), was to be brought up in
the daily use of the English tongue. At a suitable
age he was to be put to a private school in Havana
where only boys of English speech were accepted ;
but he was to pass his holidays at El Rectoret with
the staff of Cuban servants and his old Cuban nurse,
to whom a special small legacy was assigned, and
who, as housekeeper, was to administer the affairs
of that roof, where also the boy was to pass his
holidays. On reaching the age of twenty-one he
was to be paid an ample allowance, but not until
his twenty-fifth birthday was he to enter into
possession of the capital which was to be thence-
forward his absolutely. And there was the mania
of this further proviso, that if he were to leave
the island of Cuba for any reason or for however
short a time before the said twenty-fifth birthday,
he was from that moment to forfeit everything
—and no reasons given. His guardians, careful
men, and with a certain personal interest in
the affair, interpreted this so strictly that they
would not even let him have a boat to play
with off the coast, and watched his movements
strictly.

Anyone can guess the result. As the lad grew up
and knew his circumstances, it became a fixed and

burning necessity with him to travel abroad the moment he should gain his freedom.

There was yet another mania and a last proviso deriving from it. I will quote the principal words: "And I strictly charge him not to abandon but to maintain with the greatest zeal my rights over the Estate of El Pantano, whereupon is now built for the most part the town and port of Piræus, Texas, of which town and port the dues, rents, fines, etc., and all emoluments thereof I and my heirs assigns are the only true and lawful owners. With this duty I charge him under penalty of my continued disfavour . . . !" So the song ended, giving proof of yet another mania, a strong belief in old William Mallard not only in the future life, but in singular powers attaching to those enjoying that state of existence.

Perhaps if there had been any known relative, however distant, of old William Mallard, indignant members of the great legal profession might have stirred them up to contest the will, and Richard Mallard's guardians would not have been averse to undertaking so lucrative a task as its defence. But there were no such relatives, and no such action was undertaken.

And here you must understand the matter of the "Mallard Millions."

There was a doubtful tradition that old Mr. Mallard had come from England in his youth by way of the States, and there was documentary record that he had set up his business as long ago as 1910. But it was not until middle age that he began to talk mysteriously about an investment his father had made in the then worthless marsh land of El Pantano, off the lagoons on the southern Texan coast. It was thought suspicious that so long as El Pantano was a small group of fever-stricken hovels no one could remember old Mr. Mallard saying a word about it; but that when, with the development of the new fibre industry, a group of capitalists in San Antonio had begun to dredge and to drain it and turn it into a port (which they christened with the fine classic name of Piræus), when, that is, it was becoming a fortune, William Mallard woke up to it. There must have been sincerity at least in his delusion—if delusion it were —for he wasted bags of money in the Courts of the State of Texas trying to establish his claim, and always failed for lack of record. He could produce nothing but his own affirmations of his father's purchase and a few vague and conflicting allusions in letters. There were apparently no legal documents preserved, or at any rate, none forthcoming. Long before the old man's death Havana had put it down to yet another of his strange humours, and on 'Change and elsewhere the "Mallard Millions" had become a joke.

They were an established joke also, though a rather stale one, in Houston, and along the seaboard of the Gulf; with just enough interest about that joke, however ancient, to be remembered when occasion should serve, for Piræus was growing and booming.

As for young Richard, long before he was out of his teens he had grown sick of the phrase "Mallard Millions." It connoted nothing but ridicule; and as he grew up to be a lad rather shy and diffident, to whom any suggestion of being a butt was torture, he was morbidly nervous about allusions to old William's various manias and their results.

There was one point in these various manias, however, to which the boy warmly attached himself; and that was the solemn affirmation of his English descent. If his complexion was somewhat dark, it was the climate. If his accent was touched with the Colonial Spanish (and he himself was hardly aware of it), that must be put down to the use of their own idiom by his nurse in childhood and by the other domestics all about him. He carefully studied to dress and to carry himself as nearly after the English fashion as he could; and the word "Señor" addressed to him disturbed him profoundly.

He was especially careful to acquire, when he had come to that age in which very young men think everything of fashion, what he believed to be the natural phrases of the English leisured classes.

He would frequent to the very limits of discretion that Club in Havana where chance tourists from our happy Island were received, where the wealthier employees of the English houses passed their evenings, and where occasional visitors from the Bermudas or the Services were entertained.

Thus did he enrich his conversation with terms native to our rich and powerful tongue, such as "I say!" "You fellahs," "D'you know?" and the characteristic use at random of the word "What?"

Indeed, in all these uses young Mr. Mallard came to excel his masters, and an Englishman born might, were he of uneven temper, have expressed fatigue upon hearing for the fourth time such a phrase as, "I say, you fellahs, it's up to me this time, what?" and then, apologetically, "I say, you know what I mean, don't you know?"

These and others of like import were the more

emphatic for that indefinable touch of foreign accent and especially of the wide open " Ah " which lent distinction and charm, but a certain surprise to his conversation.

That proviso in the trust which kept him bound to his native island was like a leash against which the young fellow strained. The moment it lapsed, he would be off on his travels.. He would go through the States from south to north—a land of marvels. Then in due course he would sail with ancestral piety for England.

And now at last he was free ! The guardianship was ended, the trusteeship with it. He delayed only just so long as to fulfil formalities, and then was off by the first steamer for New Orleans to see the world.

Now the world is full of surprises. The first shock it gave Richard Mallard was on his landing in the sweltering damp heat of New Orleans and registering most honestly under his true name.

A brisk gentleman who had already looked at the steamer list and was comparing it with the hotel book, kindly aided by the clerk, came up to him in far too genial a fashion, said he was pleased to meet him, pulled out a notebook, and asked him for his views and forthcoming actions upon the " Mallard

Millions." The young fellow's annoyance gave him the courage to reply in suitable terms, and when this only provoked a few jocular questions on old man Mallard (the whole accompanied by rapid shorthand notes) he flamed up in answers still more suitable. The brisk gentleman being apparently delighted with such a turn of the conversation, was writing more vigorously than ever when Richard broke away, fuming over the unexpected things of the mainland. However, there was an end of that, he hoped. He consoled himself with walking abroad and seeing what there was to be seen.

But next morning, as he took up his paper at the breakfast table, he learnt more about the world. He gaped to see huge headlines, the least startling of which was :

HE REFUSED TO BE INTERVIEWED
NEW ORLEANS NEAR HELL MALLARD CLAIMS
MALLARD MILLIONS SCORES U.S.
NO HIDALGOES HERE.

There was a large snapshot photograph of himself coming down the gangway of the steamer : not a very dignified presentation. His left foot was kicking high up in the air, after the fashion of instantaneous views, and his expression was futile and bewildered. His hat was half falling off his head in the scrum.

Breakfast he could not eat. He went off immediately in the simplicity of his heart to the offices of the outrageous journal, and there protested strongly against such an abuse of liberty.

He had his reward. The evening edition had a much larger caption :

MORE MALLARD BACK CHAT.

There was no photograph this time, but a caricature to make thousands laugh, but to make the unhappy victim red with anger.

He left the city. At Birmingham he could be at peace. Little did he know! His fame had preceded him. Not one but five tormenters met him at the railway station. Wasn't he the guy Lou Davis had scored ? They followed him in procession to his hotel. When he refused to unlock his door they laid siege. When, under that force of hunger which will drive the most timorous beast from its lair, he cautiously appeared in the lounge, it was like being in the midst of a swarm of bees ; and sure enough next day he was in the papers again, with yet more violent headlines, and still funnier pictures of him dancing and screaming with rage. He fled north.

He had set the avalanche moving, and no mistake ! He had offended the Great Fraternity, and they were giving it him good.   It was a follow-on.

At Richmond he was half the front page.   In Philadelphia it was the posters, and he heard from the clerk a frightful rumour that he was going to be one of the funny things in the Topicals on the Movies.

With that cunning which the mildest will develop under persecution he designed his flight.   He fled by night in a taxi, he slept in a lost village of New Jersey, he came up next day by devious rail to New York.   That was why we saw him breathless in his trepidation trying his chance at the Travel Agency in New York.   He had had that excellent luck of finding a comfortable berth ; it had been followed by the acute misery and terror inflicted by the alert Merriman.

Now he was free.   The waters stretched out before him leading towards England, its quiet, its decency, its courtesy ; England of the books he had read and the films he had seen, where well-bred lords wearing their coronets with unaffected simplicity pass leisurely through the vast apartments of their country palaces, all opening one out of the other like a picture gallery, and are served by hosts of gigantic

liveried attendants with powdered hair. He was for
England, wherein all should be ceremonial ; where
the sentences began with " Sir " from his equals,
and ended with " Sir " from his deferential inferiors.
He felt on that quiet deck, to the soft purring of the
engines in the good summer night, as many a man
has felt who, having been forced up against a
Wagner orchestra by tyrannical women, wakes
suddenly to the blessed fact that the noise has
ceased.

The long days at sea passed easily. His recent
experiences made him shy of his fellow-beings ; but
so many of them seemed reticent and courteous,
that he was not altogether unwilling to make one
or two chance acquaintances. It would be time
enough for friends when he had put the broad band
of the Atlantic between him and that livelier kind
of society, at the memory of which he shuddered.

And the days and the nights succeeded the nights
and the days ; until at last he saw the Fastnet
Light, and the *Zeeland* was pushing eastward over
soundings and within a day of Southampton Water.

*　　　*　　　*　　　*

Forty-eight hours before the *Zeeland* had made
the Fastnet Light, Ethel (Giva), First (and Last)

Baronne de Larance, was seated at a mignonne little table of ormoulu and inlay, writing a letter, in a room in her charming villa overlooking the coast of Provence.

I am sorry to introduce yet another character so early, but I can't help myself, and anyhow, like many others, she will not trouble you long. She was a handsome woman, just on the graveyard side of fifty, with hair artificially yellow (and added to) : also an imperious carriage ; yes, and also large eye-lids, which gave her a look of veiled pride.

Her late husband, the First (and Last) Baron de Larance, had achieved his honourable position in life by services rendered to the Mediterranean Coalition—but unfortunately ill-rewarded. It was late in life that he had married Ethel (Giva) Mudgson, nearly forty years his junior : herself travelling for adventure, and without solid resources, upon the Continent of Europe. Nor had he long survived this union ; for after an attempt to increase the very inadequate fortune which political activities had brought him, he had had an accident with a revolver in the gardens of the Casino at Monte Carlo, and left Ethel (Giva), this villa, and circumstances more than distressed.

She had failed during all these long years to

harpoon a second mate—at least, a second mate
upon the only scale she would consider. But she
did not starve. The relations of the late Baron
with the Police, both under his original and modest
name of Bruyant and later in the rather low high-
politics of his middle age, were a sufficient introduction, and the lady, though continually cramped and
continually embarrassed, at least drove a trade
which is of international importance and has its
many craftsmen and women in all properly appointed
countries ; but nowhere more numerous than in
France and England, nor less numerous than in the
United States.

She was the Distributing Agent of the M. section :
the one organised by the Allied Governments for
dealing with a particular matter in which they
pooled.

And this was what she was writing, in the dear
familiar English tongue of her girlhood—it was not
going through the post, it was not going The Other
Way.

" DEAR N.G.,

"He crossed the frontier between British
Columbia and Washington State, on the 10th of
May, without regular papers. He must have got

forged papers somewhere inside. He registered
under the name of Davis when he stopped in
Omaha, and under the name of Hackenschmidt in
Chicago. He took berth 136 on the *Zeeland* under
the name of Richard Mallard. A.M.B.2 has cabled
me cypher. He is due to land at Southampton
about the 12th. Tell them to connect with him
there without fail.

" E."

The handsome, though elderly, Ethel (Giva) sighed
a contented sigh. There is payment by results over
and above the abominably insufficient salaries of
her indispensable trade, and this was a plum.
Before she fastened up the envelope she hesitated
for a moment, thinking whether to duplicate the
description for the sake of her correspondent. She
opened out the cable which had reached her four
days before. It ran thus :

TOTO MUCH BETTER SENDS YOU LOVE
MIRIAM.

which the mere toddler in cyphers can decode to :

RICHARD MALLARD BERTH 136. ZEELAND
A.M.B. 2

The rest was but a matter of referring to shipping

registers and sailings, with which the handsome, elderly, embarrassed Distributing Centre was amply supplied.

So there you have it. It was an answer to her own most urgent, anxious, three successive cables of a day before upon an unnamed person's health, and especially upon who was looking after Toto.

The Distributing Centre was satisfied. She gave the missive to her chauffeur to be taken to the station, and on from the station by the appointed person in the express for Calais. Then she went off to lose a well-deserved 10,000 francs at the tables, and so to bed.

* * * *

It is time we got back to Chap 1. And what is more, it is time that you, Unfortunate Reader, were relieved of your natural confusion and embarrassment as to what it is all about. Why all this slinking of Chap 1 through the States under false names ? Why the eagerness of the authorities in Europe, and especially in England, to discover his movements ?

To answer these questions I must first present you a certain spectacle.

Temporary seclusion of a Diplomatic Agent on the Coast of Labrador

About the time when the *Zeeland*, with the blameless Richard Mallard—Chap 2—aboard of her,
was going through the Dredged Channel into
Southampton Water, Chap 1 was seated gazing
with a fixed, unhappy stare out to sea from a
pinnacle of rock on the Labrador coast ; hoping
against hope not for a sail nor even, in these days
of Rotors, a smoke : but a ship. None appeared.

His tragic watch forcibly recalled the words of our
great Imperial poet, who, after surveying the perils
run by his Majesty's representatives (and those of
other Powers, for that matter) in Peking, the
monstrous worry of the Legation in Bucharest, and
the intolerable tedium of Teheran, has yet concluded
that :

> "No Diplomatic Agent suffers more
> Than one that is marooned in Labrador."

It is a bold thing to say of anything Imperial, but
truth is truth, and the Coast of Labrador, especially
the northern part of it, is perfectly damnable ;
nor have I ever clearly understood why Nova
Scotia, or Newfoundland, or whatever it was, wanted
it so badly as to tear it from the maternal bosom
of Quebec.

Now why was Chap 1 thus perched above the
strand, and scanning hopelessly the eastern horizon

of the Atlantic ? And who was he ? And what was he about, anyway ?

To say why Chap 1 was in this position at this date is simple enough. The intelligent reader, or for that matter a very Cretin, might have guessed it. He had been wrecked.

The *Bergen*, boasting as she did the best of the new Rotors, and well stocked with the novel but expensive Durandite, was furnished after the new fashion (which was but the return of an old one) with a single but swivel aid to progression, of the sort which educated men still call a screw, and the rest a propeller. In latitude 48.20 E. 43.15 N. (I omit the seconds, the pedantic seconds) she had dropped her screw (or propeller) like a good egg upon the Banks.

It is sometimes remarked by the disgruntled that our modern inventions always have a crab about them, and once again the disgruntled are right. The swivel screw, or propeller, saves energy, it favours rapid turning, as the single use of one of the old double propellers never could, it costs more money, and all the rest of it ; but it has this defect, that it is the devil and all to replace when you lose it. It was therefore the devil and all for the *Bergen* to replace her lost propeller, and the task was the more difficult from the fact that she carried no spare propeller aboard. The wind was from the south-east, backing south, and getting stronger. The *Bergen* helplessly drifted before it.

As to the troubles with new inventions (see above), Chalmers' patent with the Dual Process had now for more than fifteen years, indeed, since the later part of 1962, replaced the Laston affair for wireless at sea. It was much more distinct, it was less affected by climatic conditions, and it needed less power. On the other hand, if the Dual Process through some defect or jar failed to synchronise, it was hopeless. Therefore every precaution was taken to prevent the Dual Process getting such a jar and failing to synchronise. Nor did it fail by the least fraction once in twenty thousand times. But that once came off with the *Bergen*, on the same day that she dropped her screw.

Northward she drifted before the southerly rising wind; a few hours and there came down that interesting natural phenomenon, so soothing in the summer heats—a Newfoundland Bank fog. It added greatly to the anxiety of the gentleman who was responsible for the vessel, of the crew, and even of the passengers, the more intelligent of whom (and Chap 1 came very high up among these) had clearly guessed from the long absence of vibration that there was something wrong. There was. And to make matters a good deal worse, there came on the second night amid varying distant hoots, the hoot of something approaching too closely. The *Bergen's* lamentable reply puzzled the first hooter, who wirelessed vigorously. The absence of a wireless answer puzzled him more. The attempt to guess the course of the *Bergen's* hooting puzzled him worst of all. The ship appeared to be coming up north from the south. Who could be on such a course ?

They never knew. For though the collision was a violent one, the ships sheered off. The Unknown, which had taken the main shock, was badly damaged but able to crawl back to Halifax ; the *Bergen* slowly developed an increasing list to starboard and deepened a little by the head.

With the morning the fog was lighter. The wind now full south-east again was blowing more strongly. So she drifted before it for days, rolling in the trough, pumping hard and trusting that the water-tight compartments were true to their name. But the list got worse and so did the slant forward. It was on the evening of the fourth day that they decided to take to the boats : there was too much sea, but it had to be done ; and at any rate there was plenty of time to provision and water each. But as they did so the wind continually rose, and by the time they got loose it blew a full gale, with darkness falling. All that night the storm pursued them.

What happened to the other boats Chap 1 never knew. His, at any rate, had the good fortune to find, after thirty-six hours' work in front of very bad seas, the coast discernible at the second dawn.

They landed ; they camped, they built a fire with the miserable stunted stuff that grew a mile inland. Where they were they knew not, for they had no instruments ; but certainly somewhere north of Esquimaux Bay, and as certainly something human lay to the southward ; how far off they could not tell. A small party of the strongest were sent out to discover, taking with them badly grudged rations ; and Chap 1 was not of them. He discovered his pinnacle of rock on the shore half a mile from the camp, and there kept a voluntary look-out hour after hour through the very long summer days ; and saw nothing.

He was used to adventure, to hardship and peril. He took this last business grimly and firmly. He neither hoped nor despaired.

And now as to who he was ; for it is high time we were getting to that.

What his real name was I cannot tell you, for this sort of man passes under every kind of name. But I am pretty certain that he was from the boundaries of Asia, probably from Turkestan, so far as his insignificant father was concerned ; and as for his far more insignificant mother, there is no trace of her at all.

Our remote forefathers would have called him a Scythian, and he was worthy to have been suckled upon mare's milk. He was an admirable rider, but with the short stirrup ; fearless, and not so much ambitious as adventurous.

In the various revolutions on the borders of Asia since the Third great Universal Peace (the one in which Lord Peaceholme made his great fortune) after the Third Arbitration following upon the Third Debate under Unrestricted Conditions of Physical Competition (warfare had been outlawed more than a lifetime, and the very name of war had grown unfamiliar) he had floated to the top in the affairs of the Western Iranian Annihilationist Revolution and the consequent formation of the little state of West Irania in the tangle of mountains immediately south-west of the Caspian Sea.

Now West Irania thus lost amid the tangle of mountains immediately to the south-west of the

Caspian Sea was of little interest to the main governments of the world politically till quite a few years ago, even so late as 1972. Then it was that there was discovered in that little territory an exceptional, a fabulous deposit of Eremin.

When the Durand Group (as they called themselves, after the French banker) had brought out their new motive fuel Durandite, which had revolutionised the rotarian engines—especially for maritime transport—there was a crab about it : as there is a crab about all new mechanical advances (see above) In its action it was perfect. It was cheaper and cleaner than anything that had preceded it. It even gave longer life to the mechanism, and its efficacy in adding to the speed of vessels was amply proved by the sharply rising curve of naval collisions which immediately followed upon its adoption, and which, as everybody knows, continues to soar upwards. But you can't make Durandite without the essential though small proportion of Eremin. The vast resources of modern science have been taxed to their utmost to provide a substitute. We have had eremate, eremex, eremol, and a dozen other marvellous synthetic products, due to such men as Glotsch, Merof, and even Hinks ; but every

one of them in the test of practice has broken down
and Eremin remains unreplaceable.

Therefore some considerable competition for that
essential gives activity to the world ; especially is it
necessary to the fleets by water and by air which
have grown so prodigiously since the last and Third
Universal and Eternal Peace Treaty. But Eremin
(first isolated in its pure state more than thirty years
ago but made a commercial proposition less than
twenty) is exceedingly rare. It had been found in
only a few shallow deposits, which would soon be
exhausted, when there came this discovery of 1972
in West Irania.

Here was Eremin—or rather the ore from which
it could be drawn—in quantities inexhaustible and
depths so great that each new sounding discovered
a further seam.

It would seem a natural consequence of this
discovery that little West Irania should immediately
be handed over (under a mandate, of course) to one
of the greater Powers, especially as it was avowedly
Annihilationist. The Parliaments of the Great Powers
had long ago settled down into two sober parties,
Communist on the right and Anarchist on the left,
who between them maintained the Majestic Rotation of Representative Government, and against

Annihilationism they fought for their lives. **All the** great governments had an Annihilationist minority to deal with. All hated it. All were willing to render harmless the poisonous nest of West Irania. Her agents were everywhere at the ban, and their revolutionary correspondents in the great countries of the West were hunted down.

Here, again, appeared that little trick in human affairs which is always interfering with perfection. West Irania had maintained its independence through two causes : first, that the governments struggling for the Mandate had intrigued one against the other. Secondly, that one, more rash than the rest, having sent an Expeditionary Force in defence of Human Liberty and Civilisation, into the mountains of that State, the said force had been half massacred, half captured ; and the captured had been tortured to death.

Such examples are of great weight with the enlightened modern mind ; and from the moment of this military operation the attempt to get hold of the West Iranian mines had followed the methods of diplomacy rather than those of arms.

Now it frequently happens in the Diplomatic negotiations of our day that the final word lies, not with an Accredited Representative nor even with a

Second in Command, but with an Anonymous Person ; and of such a sort was Chap 1.

It lay with him what concession should be given in the matter of the West Iranian deposits, and to whom.

Every other powerful administration had first attempted the use of cajolement followed by force. In other words, they had hoped to lure among them Chap 1, and having got him, to work upon him by terror ; for he and his were still outlaws. But I am glad to say that Westminster was wiser than any other, even as it has ever been in the past and ever will be in the future. It had given Chap 1 to understand that when he should approach these shores (and they would help him to approach them with immunity) he should remain a perfectly free agent to discuss and to agree ; with a mental reservation, of course, to exercise pressure at the end, if it were absolutely necessary. But upon that last resort there was no need to insist early in the affair.

Hence the progress—the interrupted progress— of the powerful if somewhat Mongoloid Agent from West Irania to these shores. Hence also the precautions of a man not wholly devoid of suspicion to arrange that he should travel when and how he chose, in a happy *incognito*, and to land in England, when he did so land, under the same conditions. He had his mind fairly clear as to who should have the concession : it should be the British Government, and no private concern ; for the Government could pay more. But he was equally clear that there should be plenty of competition and nothing upon which they could act till he had himself received and put into a safe place the moneys which were his due, or till he had made his own person equally secure.

So there he sat on his pinnacle of rock, separated from his final action by nothing worse than the North Atlantic in front of him and Lord knows how much barren land behind.

CHAPTER III

THE Secretary of State for Home Affairs had received in due hierarchic process the news of Richard Mallard's progress across the Atlantic. For the Government, I am proud to say, had collared the Distributing Centre at a very reasonable price; and though the information upon that Gentleman had duly gone out to the Allied Governments, it had gone out a little later than to what is still called in a fine phrase " The Court of St. James." And after all, what did it matter ? Richard Mallard, the agent of West Irania, was landing on these shores first, anyhow; and the pickings would therefore naturally fall to us. Plenty of time after that to make arrangements abroad.

The Secretary of State for Home Affairs heard the news at Littleham, the new house which he had built for himself, with ample offices, a few houses and numerous cottages for his dependants, in the Surrey hills, on that belt of land reserved by the excellent Natural Beauties Protection Act of 1931 from the further encroachment of bricks and mortar. He was conferring with his secretary, by which term I mean, not his ordinary secretary (who was a young cousin destined for preferment), nor that secretary's secretary (who was a very poor man but well-bred), nor any one of the minor secretaries; but his Official Secretary, a Permanent Official of deserved importance, who, though still young (barely thirty), conducted with energy and intelligence that department for which the Secretary of State, under guidance of the Permanent Under Secretary, was responsible. Indeed, he conducted it with the greater efficiency because his superiors, the Permanent Under Secretary and the Permanent Under Secretary's Secretary, were rather concerned with the broad lines of the Department than the active details of business.

If all isn't quite clear, let me recommend Arnold's "*Our New Bureaucracy*," Piffkin and Co., 15s., pp. 274–81. Anyhow, there we have at Littleham the Secretary of State for Home Affairs, Sir Henry Hardham and his Official Secretary just summoned from the Home Office.

The Secretary of State for Home Affairs relied, very properly, upon the younger and more active brain. It would not be true to say that he knew nothing whatever about the great section of official activity over which he presided, for he had so presided over it nearly three years—in fact, ever since Mary Bullar, his cousin, the reigning Prime Minister, had formed her cabinet. But he knew that a Parliament man (and it was the first time he had held office) caught up in the intense intellectual activity of the House of Commons could not master the working of a Ministry which controlled all England, and needed to rely upon the experience of men who had discharged their duties continuously under all governments for many years. And of these his Official Secretary was the most reliable and the most competent. He had been assured so by the Office itself, and by his colleague—that omniscient Lady Caroline Balcombe, Secretary of State for Foreign Affairs.

The Secretary of State for Home Affairs was a gentleman—he had lineage behind him—six generations of squires—and was therefore naturally of the Communist party, the spiritual descendants of the old Moderates, themselves the spiritual descendants of the old Unionists, themselves the spiritual descendants of the old Conservatives, themselves the spiritual descendants of the old Tories : for, thank heaven, there is no breach of continuity in our institutions !

Indeed, he had a simpler faith than most men of
the world (if he could be called a man of the world)
in what he was proud to call the "Principles of
Communism"; and, unlike too many of his colleagues,
he felt a real spiritual separation between himself
and the Anarchist Party, which was at the time in
Opposition ; though that Party contained many of
his relatives and not a few of his intimate friends.
As for the small body of wild men, those "Annihilationists" who had crept into the House by some
accident at the last election, he refused to consider
their existence, and in his contempt for them he
had behind him the mass of his fellow-citizens.
"For," as his cousin the Prime Minister, Mary
Bullar, had finely said in her recent speech at
Nottingham, "there is something un-English about
the very word Annihilationist. The good old
English party names of Anarchist and Communist
are good enough for us."

So that day, as he walked across the lawn of his
new house at Littleham, with his Official Secretary,
his whole reticent character was presented. His
long, gentle face (still distinguished by those ample
whiskers, the fashion for which had been revived
in his long past youth of the 1940's) grew somewhat
livelier in the midst of the discourse. His tone

which fools described as lugubrious, but his friends as resembling an ecclesiastical chant, rose and fell in excellent illustrations of the duty before them. He could speak with authority; for his position, like that of so many in the Communist Party, was a family one. His great-grandfather had been in one of Gladstone's cabinets before the flood, and his nephew and heir, already enjoying talents not unlike his own, had been adopted as candidate for a safe constituency, unfortunately at some distance from the metropolis.

He had opened the subject of Mallard's approaching landing with the remark that nothing was more important in secret negotiations than preventing them from leaking out. Whoever was to meet Mallard and discover his movements must be a trustworthy man, lest any hint of their intentions and the Envoy's identity should appear in the Press. The Official Secretary had acquiesced in this view, and had even suggested respectfully that it might be unwise to discuss the matter before domestics at meals. The Home Secretary nodded.

" When a secret is to be observed," he said, " it is of the first importance. Mind you," he added, suddenly halting in his steps, and fixing his younger companion, " of the *first*—I will go further and say

5

The Home Secretary reciting the qualities required in a Secret Agent

even of the *last*—importance, that one should pick
one's agents carefully."

Once more the Official Secretary agreed.

"Many an important transaction," continued his
Chief, in solemn but clear and bell-like tones, "has
been ruined by the choice of a babbler. What does
history show us ? " he continued, in that increasing
fluency which all his dependants and associates knew
and many dreaded. "History shows us that nearly
every enterprise which has failed, has failed through
the choice of the wrong agents. Take the case of
the Armada . . ."

But his companion was secretly unwilling to take
the case of the Armada, or to waste any more time.
He allowed the speech to run on; then, like the
cautious man who waits for a lull in the traffic
before he crosses the Strand, he butted in just as
the Great Statesman had got as far as the first
return of the Spanish Fleet after the storm in
the Bay of Biscay.

"I thought of Palmer," he said briefly.

"Palmer ? " said the Home Secretary, who heard
the name for the first time. "Oh, Palmer. Yes.
Palmer! Palmer will do very well! You will
generally notice about these men who are efficient
in secret service of any kind that they have a sort

of native discretion. They do not seem to have the same desire to communicate with their fellows as have other men ; and yet they give no suspicious impression of reticence in their conversation. Now I remember a man . . ."

The Official Secretary waited, and then cut in again at a breather :

" I have taken the liberty of telling them to wire to Palmer ; shall I telephone to him and confirm ? "

" Yes," said the Home Secretary genially. " Telephone them by all means. I am sure you could not have made a better choice. In fact, it was my intention to have suggested Palmer myself, when you mentioned him. These coincidences are very strange ! But no one can deny that they happen. I remember my grandfather, when I was but a child, telling me that Mr. Gladstone said to his father . . . "

Harris pulled out his watch suddenly.

" Sir Henry," he said, " I shall only just catch him. He's only waiting at the office till six o'clock," and he ran off.

The Home Secretary, having no one else to talk to, turned back to the house, talking to himself, but in a low and discreet voice; for he was dimly aware that the habit gives one a ridiculous appearance. He strolled towards the house with his hands clasped behind him, muttering an imaginary speech . . .

" . . . I agree with all that the Right Honourable Gentleman has said—the Right Honourable and Gallant Gentleman, I should say—Lady, I mean— and I should myself be in complete agreement with him—and I mean her—were it not for another consideration which, if I am not mistaken . . ."

At that moment he ran into a fine Corinthian pillar that flanked his Adams door. It hurt him. But the finely-bred nose bled only slightly. It was soon staunched and he was ready to join his peers within. The long duty of the day was accomplished. He had picked the very man; Palmer, the astute Palmer, was under orders to meet the *Zeeland* at Southampton and to deal with the situation as delicate occasion might demand.

*　　　*　　　*　　　*

A very pleasant, blue-eyed young man, clean-shaven, curly-headed, candid, fair, and all the rest of it, and, by the way, properly dressed, without excess, loosely and in clothes not too new, passed the ticket collector at Southampton West and nodded genially. Also did the ticket collector at

Southampton West very respectfully salute him—
for he was not unknown.

There is no mystery about his name. His name
was Palmer, and a more cheerful, straightforward
companion you would not meet in a day's march.
The New Section (K.K.) of the Special Intelligence
Department (B) was proud of him.

Young as he was—twenty-eight—he had acquired
all the tricks of the trade. By which you may
gather that he was open, of good deportment, and
that his laugh was the only infectious thing about
him. Also, in spite of his salary, which was still
under seven hundred a year, though rising, he had
acquired every gesture of leisure in the muscles of
his face, in his walk, in the contented expression of
his eyes. He was marked for promotion. He
already knew things ; and he was a youth who
could use his pull.

I love to dwell on such characters. He was
married, and he already had one charming little
child, who, let us hope, would, when he grew up,
be in the Government Service as well, or perhaps
(if his father did exceptionally well) a company
promoter and a peer—who knows ? The villa was
—so far—at Golders Green.

Young and happy Mr. Palmer walked out into

the June sunlight and hired a taxi. He did well over it, for the British taxpayer paid. He drove to the offices of the Southern Railway, near the docks.

Here also he was greeted with respect by the aged watcher at the gate, to whom his features had lately become especially familiar, and he nodded genially in return. A thought occurred to him.

" Pay the taxi, Johnson," he said ; and that was 2s. 6d. up for Mr. Palmer and 2s. 6d. down against you and me, the taxpayers ; but what is that among so many ?

For Mr. Palmer was very careful in making out the whole list of his expenses, and the taxi at Southampton came into that list.

Before he went on to the private office, he turned for a moment to sniff the half-tide air and to enjoy the sunlight. You would have had some difficulty if you had seen him standing thus to decide whether he was Eton and New College, Eton and Balliol, Winchester and Balliol, Harrow and Balliol, Winchester and New College, Eton and King's, Winchester and Trinity, Rugby and Sid Sussex, Repton and Worcester, or even Radley and Teddy Hall. And your hesitation would have been natural, for he was none of these things. And it was as well. For it left him unrecognised by those whom it was his duty to observe.

But no matter. He was an industrious servant of that great machine whereby the society of Europe in general, and of England in particular, is kept on its tottering legs.

The official inside the little office received him with even more deference than had the janitor. They talked genially about the allocation of Mr. Richard Mallard to a particular compartment in the special boat train up to London, and of a particular seat in the dining car.

"I hope he won't kick," said jolly young Mr. Palmer.

"I don't see how he could," said the official. "I'll see that he is put to the right place by the Shepherd, and locked in; and then they can let you in at the last moment."

"Oh, by the way, I shall want to take a bag. I can't be bothered to bring a bag down every time I come." ·

"I'll see that the porter has one ready for you."

"Yes, and please have the label on it with the name of some New York Hotel. No, wait a moment. I forgot. Yes, I'll say I was ill on the boat. No, that won't work." He thought for a

moment. " Just put a Paris Hotel label on it.
You've got plenty of 'em ? "

" Plenty. What hotel ? "

" Oh, the Ritz," said Mr. Palmer, yawning.
" They've all heard of the Ritz," and he laughed
merrily. " I'll have the bag sent back."

The official rang a bell. The watcher appeared.

" Berry," he said, " get one of the new bags with
gold fittings. Have we any Ritz labels—Paris
Ritz ? "

" Yes, sir, a fresh bundle from the printers last
week."

" Well, paste it on the bag and put on a chalk
Customs mark somewhere and bring it here. I'm
sorry to give so much trouble, but you'll have it
back as I said."

" Of course," said the official, " of course. You
know, Mr. Palmer," he went on musingly, " I don't
know whether to admire you or to scold you. You're
the only one that won't be bothered to bring a bag
down. It doesn't seem so much trouble, after all.
However, we shall always have one for you."

" Yes," said the genial Mr. Palmer, rising again
and stretching his arms, " let *them* work. I hate
carrying things about. It's bad enough to have to
take it to the cab from the London terminus. Your

people can collect it to-morrow at the department. I'll address it. When does the *Zeeland* come in ? "

" She was signalled leaving Cherbourg at four. She'll berth about six, and we'll get the train off before half-past seven."

" So that I shall have to eat that uneatable dinner of yours after all," said Palmer.

It was the official's sore point.

" Mr. Palmer," he said, " I don't understand this way of talking. It's just a thing that people say against the Company because it's the fashion to say it. What better can you have ? " he went on, growing enthusiastic. " Gravy soup. Boiled turbot, *pré salé,* and the very best Canadian cheese ? "

" Oh, never mind," answered Palmer. " I know one place in Southampton where a man can eat ; it's Cortoni's, and I'm going there now. I always eat two hours before getting on to one of your trains. Now look here ; it mustn't go off until I turn up—and I shall turn up at the very last minute, so that your man may have an excuse for unlocking that door."

" Right, Mr. Palmer, I'll send the bag up to Cortoni's," said the official. " May I offer you a glass of Madeira ? "

It was the common ritual. The Madeira was good

and Madeira is an excellent wine to take a little
before eating. Each of these two men drank his
small glass, and so parted in harmony—each having
aided the vast machinery of government.

The *Zeeland* forged her way through a sea still
calm—it had been calm all the way over from New
York—past the Needles, past the Shingles, up the
Solent and into her berth. Mr. Palmer was having
a very good and reasonable meal, after the Italian
fashion, and he drank with it, not the common
Chianti, for which you and I would have paid only
3s. 6d., but first-rate wine at 8s. : your 8s. and mine.

* * * *

Richard Mallard, as he stood by the boat train
at the Quay, was in a happy mood. He felt like
one meeting an expected though as yet unseen
friend ; and so a man ought to feel when he comes
young and free from care and with enough money,
by the delightful calm of an English June evening
into a new land, and is invigorated by the architecture
of Southampton.

Everything pleased him. The courtesy of those
poorer than himself, the shouts and the bustle, the
sham luxury of the carriages—but what especially
pleased him was the way in which he was put into

the train, in a sort of semi-royal fashion, by a person in uniform who gazed upon him in a paternal fashion, and guided him to an exact goal after a manner which had well earned him (on the reverse or official side of his life) his title of the Shepherd.

" You will have the compartment to yourself, sir," he said. " We haven't got a great many people travelling ; it's not a very crowded train to-night, sir." (Again "Sir"—oh, how pleasant was that word "Sir!" How often would it be repeated?) " I think these two bags was all you had in hand with you, sir? I've seen about your registered luggage, sir."

Richard Mallard wondered to himself at what a tariff such kindness should be rewarded. He decided that five dollars was too much and two dollars too little, and he handed the Shepherd ten shillings. It was but a trifle compared with what the Shepherd received from an intelligent country for his services, but it was accepted with dignity and gratitude. The little green paper changed hands ; the Shepherd locked the door, touched his gorgeous cap and made off with majesty ; and there was Richard, enjoying a comfortable seclusion.

How unfamiliar the furnishing all was, and how dignified : the dark polished wood, the deep leather the hanging arm rests like those he had seen in pictures of old coaches, and all the rest of it! How traditional and how soothing! He had done well to fly from the haste of the New World. Here he would be at peace. He was pleased to see that, not content with locking him in, the Shepherd had pasted over the window against the platform side a label with the word "Reserved" in large red letters.

He sank back for a long repose, occupying as master that small domain of which he would be for two hours the unique lord. The Shepherd passed again for a moment, and nodded with a mixture of kindness and deference which was delightful to the young man's soul. One pompous shouting man waved a flag, another pompous shouting man shouted "All Clear There!" Further pompous shouting men shouted other things—when suddenly, just as the train was moving, someone who was not the Shepherd, but in uniform, appeared suddenly at the door of the compartment, unlocked it, and there bounced in breathless, holding a bag marked "E. W." with a prominent label of the Paris Ritz and a Customs mark, the heartening personality of Mr. Palmer. The train was gathering speed, a porter slammed the open door as it

passed him, and there they found themselves, one
opposite the other, and Mr. Palmer apologising
profusely.

"I am really extremely sorry," he said. "I
almost missed the train, and they put me in where
best they could. It's entirely my fault. I don't
think they saw that reserved notice. If you'll only
wait a moment I'll find a place somewhere else."

He spoke too quickly, and seemed out of breath
with running. Richard Mallard was far too courteous
to turn him out.

"On the contrary," he said, "it will be delightful
to have a companion. You see, I'm new to this
country," he added ingenuously.

"Are you ?" said Palmer, with intense interest.
"I should never have guessed it. You're not an
American ?"

"No, not exactly," said Richard.

"I've just come from France. I got on at
Cherbourg."

"I didn't see you."

"I think I saw you for a moment, but I can't
be sure. Really I'm extremely sorry . . ."

"No, not at all, I assure you. It's lovely country,"
he went on. People from overseas who rush through
South England like this for the first time always

use that simple phrase, and Mr. Palmer was grateful to heaven to find his charge so true to type. Also he noticed the slight indefinable foreign accent. Also he noticed the initials " R. M." on the other's handbags. Also the boots, the very pointed boots. He took it all in, with eyes round and innocent as a female cinema star's.

The face puzzled him. That mild, innocuous air, that small soft moustache, and those gentle, almost pathetic eyes. It was not what he had been led to look out for. But then . . . it was the business of these gentry to look the part and to act it well.

He kept the conversation lively. The passenger from off the *Zeeland* replied with frankness and a juvenile curiosity. He was ready to talk about himself, apparently at any length, and his zeal was to learn more of the lovely fields and the old buildings of the land through which they passed.

Then did Mr. Palmer let her all out, and described in a fashion Richard Mallard could well understand not only the beauty but the history of what they saw, and before Winchester was passed they were fast friends. Immediately after that city, as they climbed the chalk hills, and a sad-faced, determined waiter had summoned them to the dining car, Richard Mallard had already a feeling

Enthusiasm of Mr. Palmer for the Scenery of South England

of home ; and Mr. Palmer the feeling of a man
who has caught a man out from leg, and not a
driven ball at that, but an easy lob.   So both were
satisfied.

All during the meal they exchanged engrossing
confidences, and Richard Mallard learned all that
Mr. Palmer desired that Richard Mallard should
believe him to be ; and Mr. Palmer learned all that
Richard Mallard really was—which Mr. Palmer
himself did not for one moment believe.

They had finished dinner.   The broad daylight
was turning mellow though the sun had not set.
They were at their coffee—Mallard still talking
volubly of Cuba, of his home, of his voyage.

" Don't smoke the cigars here," said Palmer.
" Wait a moment, and I'll go back and get one out
of my bag.   I've got some I like, and you might
like them too.   You people from the West Indies
are hard to please, but I think I know a cigar.   I'll
be back in a second."

" Don't take the trouble," said Richard Mallard,
rising, overwhelmed by so much kindness.

" No, no ; you wouldn't know where they are,"
(they were in his pocket at that very moment) ;
" I assure you, I'm delighted," said Palmer, gently
pushing him back into his seat.   And so he was.

6

He went at top speed through the train to the abandoned compartment. It would be a pity to allow a suspicious gap in time. He tried, like lightning, the larger leather bag of his amiable companion: it was locked. He tried the small despatch case: it was open — but it was disappointing. There were no "papers." There was a magazine, a detective novel, a map of England, and a guide book, and a spare handkerchief, but nothing that you could call "papers." Unless—stay, yes, here was something.

It was a set of half-finished notes. Time pressed, but Mr. Palmer had a first-rate memory. He photographed on that memory of his the names jotted down.

"*London, the Titanic. Stratford. Name of the Hotel in the Lakes : The Black Horse.*

Then Scotland.

Continent can wait."

So the notes ran.

He snapped the clasps and hurried back to the dining car, pulling out of his pocket as he went that case of cigars which had been lying there all the time.

" I've got them," he said. " Hope I haven't kept you waiting."

They smoked in peace, still discussing Cuba and

English **scenery** alternately till it was nearly dark.
As the train rolled through immense London in the
gloaming, Richard Mallard showed an excitement
and interest which moved his companion to a real
admiration. He had never seen the thing better
done! But when the traveller recognised the
Houses of Parliament over the water against the
red sky ("and so like the picture"), when he
shouted like a schoolboy at the discovery, Mr.
Palmer thought the note a little forced.

"I can drop you at your hotel, if you like," he
said. "It's on my way."

"Thank you," said Richard Mallard. "We'll
share. It's the Titanic. I'll be glad to be shown
the way. I wirelessed for a room, so they're
expecting me."

At the Titanic Mr. Palmer lingered just long
enough to hear the number of the room, then he
shook hands warmly and was off westward to drop
the borrowed bag at the Department and then to
his Club.

There, in the writing-room of the Junior Loyalists'
Club, did the efficient Mr. Palmer prepare for a
business that might mark a step in his career.
First he tore off the unmarked sheet of a double
piece of notepaper, held it up to the light to see that

there was no watermark, and wrote thereon a **report** with careful thought and frequent pauses.

> " The description exactly tallies, and the luggage is marked R.M. It consists in two new leather bags, one with a New York maker's name, and both apparently bought together. The larger luggage will follow to the Titanic where he has room 227, no bath. I had no opportunity of opening the larger bag. The despatch case was unlocked, so in any case he would not have had anything of importance in it, but I thought it worth noting a paper on which was jotted something of an itinerary. He doesn't propose to go to Paris until he has gone first to some Stratford. No indication which Stratford, or Stratford might possibly be a man's name. He has an appointment to meet someone in the Lakes at a hotel called the ' Black Horse.' "

Here he rose from the writing table, went to the shelves where were the books of reference and looked up in a road book the " Black Horse " (or " Black Horses ") of the Lake District. He found but one which seemed of sufficient importance, and he went back to write . . . .

> " It would seem to be the ' Black Horse ' at Culldon on Dale Water ; but it may, for purposes of a secret meeting, be the little public house of the same name on the road from Kendal to Windermere. Next he goes to Scotland, but there is no indication as to where in Scotland. Does Scotland mean Worsing ?

He is passing as a Cuban of English descent and gives minute details of a home in Cuba to add to the impression."

There followed a very good and full précis of the conversation he had held with his grateful companion.

At the end he risked a warning on the man's excellent acting, specially explaining his unbroken air of simplicity, his remarkably good and familiar English (with a very slight accent) and his absolute consistency in his assumed rôle.

He read the document over very carefully, thoughtfully adding and correcting here and there. Then he laboriously made out a fair copy, put the original into an inner pocket, and the fair copy into an envelope, which he sealed and took himself to the Department, and handed to the colleague who kept watch during the earlier part of the night, before the change over.

As he left the Department Big Ben was striking eleven. He got into the Tube for Golders Green with high satisfaction in his soul. He had done well.

CHAPTER IV

LADY CAROLINE BALCOMBE was by every tradition of her great family (she was a Baugh of Woolstone by birth) attached to the Anarchist party, of which her own father had been a sort of second leader in the early middle of the twentieth century. But indeed, that whole group of hereditary talent had always been inclined to the more democratic interpretation of our public affairs.

She was still young as political life goes, or at least young for the high office she occupied, only entering her sixty-fifth year ; and her tall, slight but energetic and highly distinguished figure was perhaps that most familiar to the masses in our public life. Her whole record had been a succession of triumphs, with none of those checks and temporary eclipses which seem, with most people, to be a necessary part of Parliamentary careers. Save at the moment of Charles Balcombe's death (a shock which withdrew her from public activities for nearly a week) there had been for over thirty years no interruption to political activities which had been of the highest service to the nation.

For one thing, she had inherited that gift of compromise and moderation which happily prevented the Anarchist party from falling into the hands of its extremists. There was perhaps no one more hated by the handful of Wild Men in her own party or by the small separate group of Annihilationists.

There is a famous phrase of hers with which all will be familiar, but which I am proud to recall here in her honour. It was delivered in the great meeting at Bristol, as long ago as 1952, when it looked as though the party was going to be " bolted " by the violent mob protests and dangerous demagogy of Beddington against the Industrial Conscription Bill. The high soprano voice which rang out like a silver trumpet on that occasion, and the words it found to express the very soul of Statesmanship, will hardly be forgotten so long as representative government endures :

" I am as profoundly attached to Anarchy, and to all the principles of Anarchy, as any woman or man here present. But the only Anarchy I know is an Anarchy to be achieved by Constitutional Means."

Lady Caroline Balcombe pinning her Faith in Anarchy to the Constitutional Instincts of the British People

The great statement stands as a landmark in the recent history of our country.

In spite of being in Opposition for so many years, she had now been attached (under the well-established formula of Personal Coalition), since its formation in 1976, to the Communist Ministry, of which Mrs. Bullar was the energetic chief. The arrangement was a sheer public necessity, for one may honestly say that Lady Caroline had become indispensable as Secretary of State for Foreign Affairs.

Why this should be so it would be difficult to say, though all her contemporaries felt it in their bones. To this general consensus I know of no exception, and even Lord Arthur Baugh, her brother, will agree with my judgment. She was one of those women of whom one feels that they occupy naturally and inevitably a certain place in politics. She was of those who have one essential function ; and the management of England's external relations was hers.

It was not her short experience with Bernstein's mission, in her early youth, nor even her considerable mass of writing upon European and American diplomacy in the Reviews. It was not even the authoritative position which she had taken on the rare occasions when she spoke in debate upon the international position of Britain, though she had certainly distinguished herself quite early in her Parliamentary career as a private member in her speech upon the long past American and Canadian Alliance against Japan. Her defence of Tuffler's policy in aiding Japan against that Alliance put into form, clear cut and convincing, what all were thinking more or less confusedly, but what none had so formally expressed.

" Though Mother and Daughter differ—yea, even with heat—are they not Mother and Daughter still ? "

The present Archbishop, then Moderator of the Christian Liberty Churches, has confessed to me that he was moved to tears by the sublimity of the metaphor.

Many years after, when she was in Opposition, after a long and brilliant Under Secretaryship, she had intervened in debate with memorable force upon one of the gravest crises in Imperial Destiny. The nation had passed through the great ordeal of Indian Emancipation, and might have been thought too exhausted for further emotion, when it was shaken to its depths over the so-called " Cession " of Ceylon. Few were clear-headed enough to perceive that the political control of the Island was a mere convention, and that the reality of the situation lay in our banking system and investments there, all of which were safeguarded. Crude, superficial judgment would have risked all—even the Italian Understanding—rather than agree, and once again it was her power of metaphor which proved of such inestimable value to her country.

" Because a jewel is mine, may I not give it to a friend ? And if that friend " (she added) " is better fitted to wear the trinket than I, is the act not fitting as well as justified ? " Whether, indeed, the Italian administration of Ceylon (under Mandate, of course) has justified the hopes held out by its advocates may be debated, but no one can remain unaffected by the brilliance of Lady Caroline's plea, a brilliance made the more effective by the superb delivery in which it was made. And how strikingly the voice trembled upon the parallel of a young beauty better fitted to be adorned than a woman of maturer years !

Yet, I say, it was none of these things which had given Lady Caroline her inevitable place as Foreign Minister ; it was that something which cannot be defined and by which we know that a certain public task is exactly suitable to one particular public woman, and to no other. Even the contrast between her soprano and the contralto of her Chief helped to emphasise that truth.

Now that she had occupied the Foreign Office for eight years (five under the late Anarchist administration, three in this), the mental and spiritual energy inhabiting that frail body seemed in no way diminished even under the burden of her great office ; and in the most difficult crisis of the Coalition, when she had successfully defended to the Cabinet the policy of her Permanent Under-Secretary, Callingham, and had agreed to pay the reparations demanded by the Islamic Council after the Bouzi Beg incident, it was she, once more, who had turned the scale.

*   *   *   *

She was seated before the great desk in the large, cool room which was such a refuge from the summer heat outside, holding in her left hand the tortoise-shell and gold lorgnette which is so familiar in her popular portraits, and going carefully line by line over the Memorandum propped up before her. Callingham was at her right hand, standing

Lady Caroline Balcombe plumbing the Depths of
European Affairs

respectfully as is the custom when a man of his position has a Lady for his Chief.

> "It is essential to remember that West Irania is technically and by Treaty an independent and sovereign state. And this is not only a question of protocol— any hint at another state of affairs would at once end the negotiations. To act as though no one else was concerned but the man who, as we know, can speak for the so-called 'Government' of West Irania, is the key of the situation. The whole world knows, of course, that the Asiatic Federation is in practice master. It is one of those arrangements of which we had the first example in the constitution of the United States, copied from our own treatment of Imperial problems, in what may be called the transition period, where the paramount power leaves its sub-ordinates free to act to its own advantage, though it will at once take up the quarrel if that subordinate be attacked. The principle is illogical, and perhaps immoral, but . . . . ."

At this point Lady Caroline stopped and looked up at her Permanent Under-Secretary.

" Isn't all that redundant ? " she said.

" Yes, if you think it so," said Callingham ; and Lady Caroline's little gold pencil went steadily through the whole paragraph except the first two lines.

" Now," she said, smiling up at him again, " we can come down to brass tacks."

She read on :

" It is on account of these relations and also on account of the hostile feelings abroad against West Irania since the last Annihilationist Massacres that this emissary has been despatched so secretly. It is one of those instances, which are becoming increasingly numerous in recent years, where the openly accredited representatives of a Government have no real authority to negotiate, and where a secret agent carefully preserving his identity from the knowledge of the public has the final word.

" We know from experience that under these circumstances a verbal agreement is a better foundation for all that is to follow than the formal documents that will later be exchanged. In this case Azaphan has crossed the Pacific as a commercial traveller under the name of Barinov. He came to the United States under the name of Davis, registered in Chicago in the name of Hackenschmidt and we are informed by the Home Office that he has landed in England at Southampton under the name of Mallard. The Home Office have sent a man down to follow and report, and it is to them the Government must turn, in the first instance, for information before proceeding further.

" Two things would now seem to be essential : first, that if possible some definite conclusion should be come to with him upon the concession of the Eremin deposits for not less than fifty years. The thing is of such moment we can afford to be generous both with the man himself in his private capacity and with the State for which he acts ; secondly, if he delays proceedings with the object of an ' auction '—in order to obtain the highest terms—we must intervene before he can grant the concession to any private firms. The two principal competing interests are the Delisport and Worsing groups, and each is but a subsidiary of foreign interests.   If the negotiations fail, force must intervene.

" When I say intervene, I mean going to full lengths. We must find cause to have him arrested on some trivial ground, and then hold over him as a part of our bargaining power an enquiry into the part he took by correspondence in the shipping riots five years ago. If he is at liberty after showing indisposition to accept the very generous offers of the British Government, we can hardly doubt it will mean the capture of the Eremin deposits by commercial groups which are ultimately German and American."

Lady Caroline wagged her head decisively. " Too long ! Too long ! " she said.

" I'll take it back and try to make it shorter, if you like," said Callingham respectfully.

" N-no," mused his superioress with the pencil at her lip. " I think I can do that," and she first thoughtfully cancelled all he had written before and then jotted down at the foot of the document :

" To be got hold of immediately and clinched.   If he wriggles, lag."

" There," she said, leaning back and smiling again pleasantly at her Permanent Official, satisfied at a task accomplished, " I think that corks the bottle ? "

She pulled a bit of paper towards her and held her pencil delicately in the air. She was considering the incapacity of the Home Secretary, Sir Henry

Hardham, and the necessity of using him none the less.

" Cally," she said, " I think we must jog Mary, and make her jog that old idiot Henry."

She looked up and smiled once more at her Permanent Secretary in a bewitching manner, born of many years' experience—of nearly sixty years' experience—for in the rank to which the leading families of the great Anarchist party belongs that sort of thing begins in the nursery.

" I don't think the P.M. will want much jogging," said Callingham, not without respect for both parties.

" Let us say, then," mused the Foreign Secretary, with her head delicately on one side, " direction, guidance, savage jerk at the bit, what ?—yes ! "

Callingham's was a duteous smile.

" We'll put her through it," said his chief briefly : " ring, Cally, ring."

Higden, Permanent Civil Servant of the XVIIth class, appeared at the door.

" We want the Prime Minister," said Callingham, as to a serf, and a passable number of minutes later the apparatus buzzed and Lady Caroline applied her long-experienced but still delicate ear. Then she gave tongue.

7

"Mary, you've got to get hold of Henry and make that old jackass see this Mystery Man himself." So spoke the refined soprano voice, in the manner of one who, though not technically chief, could put a hand on the reins of affairs.

She listened to the short contralto reply, then spoke again :

"Kick ? Of course he'll kick ! He's never done a stroke of work in his life, and he doesn't want to ! But this time it's chip in or bust. Delisport will be on to it, and so will Worsing. We've got to get our foot in the door *first*."

She paused for a second reply. Then she went on, a couple of notes higher. "Oh, don't bother as to how I know ! The thing's obvious. Do you suppose a man like Delisport wouldn't be on to it ? We've got to be twenty-four hours ahead.

"Now don't be sticky, Polly. Just ring up Cousin Harry and put him through it. After all, we've got all the details here ; it's our department, ain't it ? . . . Well, his department's got the job of holding the lad, and it's up to him to get the stuff and let you know at once—as soon as it can be worked. Delisport may be on to him before we know. . . . When you've

Mary Bullar, Prime Minister of England, C.B.,
D.B., D.B.E., C.F., B.F., etc., etc. (From
the pencil sketch by Leslie in the Publicity
Department)

seen Henry come over and tell me. I'll wait for you."

And that was that.

*   *   *   *

Mrs. Bullar was an ideal Prime Minister. I know it is a hackneyed phrase to use of her—it has been used by everybody else a thousand times—but it is true.

She was in successful contrast with her predecessor, Lady Sarah Palasch, who ought really never to have been chosen Head of the Party, what with her family troubles and her own personal failings, let alone the distractions she suffered from the vagaries of her daughter, and all that wretched story about her present fifth husband and the cheque. Now, under the firm hand of Mary Bullar, England could repose. She was a strong, capable woman, hardly fifty, with that new style of square face which has been imported from a higher and greater civilisation ; a most determined mouth, and steady, deciding eyes which even before she spoke put confidence into the wavering and the fear of God into the weak.

It is among the latter, I fear, that we must count the Home Secretary, with whom the Prime Minister

was closeted. They two alone occupied the big
room of the great ferro-concrete buildings in the
Sumerio-Aztec manner in Downing Street (still called
" Number Ten ").

" It's no good arguing," said Mary Bullar.
" Someone has got to give the order, and I have
given it. My dear fellow," she added, pushing her
chair back from the table, crossing her legs (or
rather ankles, for she had Presence), " it's not
a thing I like saying, but if you do not care for
the duties of your office, you are always free to
resign."

The Home Secretary caressed his right-hand
whisker for a moment.

" The resignation of a Cabinet Minister is a very
serious thing," he murmured : " serious for him, and
serious for the country. It has been well remarked
in the essay on that great and good man the first
Duke of Wellington, which Purbery has just written,
that . . . "

" Yes. I know," cut in Mrs. Bullar shortly. And
as she said it she got up from her chair. " We'll
take that as read. I can't depend upon any inter-
mediate reports, and the less people in this so much
the better. You must have him to your house,
yourself, and you must see how far he'll go ; then

*Firm attitude of Mary Bullar towards her
Home Secretary*

you must report to me.   After that, we can decide.
But not before."

What a long way the political system has travelled
since the old days—yet not so very many years ago
—when Prime Ministers were but the colleagues of
their fellows in the Cabinet, and when they would
sometimes be actually so weak as to submit essential
public actions to majority votes!

" So that's settled," she went on.   " Did you come
in your motor ? "

" Yes," said the unfortunate man, dismally glaring
in his mind at the prospect of an interview, alone,
with a dangerous international criminal and quasi-
diplomat to boot.   He !   Henry Hardham !   And
HE had to draw him out !   He !   Henry Hardham !
How could he draw anybody out ?   Well, there was
always Harris to consult.

" Then give me a lift to Caroline's—I'm going
there to arrange the French correspondence about
it."

The Home Secretary deposited her at Caroline
Balcombe's house, where that Indispensable was
waiting, a little impatient, for the Prime Minister's
arrival.   He drove on to his own house, and telephoned for the Mallard Papers to be brought to
him : they were not to forget the photograph

snapped at Waterloo, of which he had heard, but which he had not yet seen.

As he ran over the notes, the task seemed less formidable. The conversation of the man was well reported, he seemed to be quiet; he would even pass, they said, for an Englishman, or at any rate for a colonial. And the photograph clinched it. It was a very pleasant, open face. The more dangerous, of course, but the better for a party such as he had to meet. It took him a good deal over an hour to make up his mind. He telephoned to Harris.

"Harris, I've got to meet this man at dinner. Can you suggest anything? . . . Who's Elizabeth? . . . Oh, your sister,—yes, of course. Your sister. . . . But she doesn't know anyone who knows him? Oh, yes, of course—the man you're keeping at the hotel for the moment . . . Railton? Yes, capital. . . . That'll do very well. If Railton gives your sister luncheon, then she can ask him to dinner to meet my niece, and then my niece can ask him to dinner and I'll be there. . . . That's a very good idea. . . . I'm glad you think three steps isn't too sudden. . . . You know I was going to ask him myself . . . directly . . . no, no, no. . . . Yes, yes, I agree—it wouldn't have done. You're quite

right. . . . I remember a case of the same kind
in the last administration. . . . Very often in this
world the simplest plan is the best. . . . Burke has
a remarkable saying about the virtue of direct
action in a public man, and . . . Are you there,
are you there ? . . . I say, Exchange, you've cut
me off ! "

The agony of disappointed recitative played for a
moment over the whiskered and suffering face of
the Home Secretary. He gave it up as a bad job,
and hung up the receiver. Anyhow, that was all
settled.

And sure enough, towards the end of the week,
the hop, skip and jump had been taken. Richard
Mallard had been nobbled by Railton, who had passed
him on to Harris and his sister, who had passed
him on to the niece and there he was—and the Home
Secretary's niece was giving her dinner, and the
Great Minister himself sat facing Mr. Richard Mallard
across the table. That young gentleman was
awed and bewildered. He had lived in a three
days' whirl, marvelling at the hospitality of the
English and deciding there must be something
popular about him to land him so swiftly in such
company. The grandeur of the House appalled
him.

Yet the dinner was a small and quiet one, specially designed to rope in Envoys of doubtful birth : and the Home Secretary was in familiar surroundings, which eased his nervousness. During dinner he thought it his duty to study the face of the secret Envoy of West Irania. He had always read that this was what one had to do before approaching mysterious people ; indeed, he remembered a very striking passage in the Memoirs of Sir Arthur Holton —it was in the second volume, if he remembered rightly . . . etc., etc.

But the watching of the Dark Unknown as a preliminary process was not easy. It involved a game of Peep-bo round an enormous Renaissance ewer of silver gilt, adorned with gods and goddesses of the brawnier type ; and sometimes when the Home Secretary leaned to the left, poor Mallard— very shy in such exalted company—would lean to his left to talk to the lady on that side ; and sometimes when he leaned to the right, Mallard would be turning to the lady on his right—having already caught the see-saw trick which is law at the Tables of the Great.

However, Sir Henry did manage to get one or two fairly good looks at the Enigma—with the very natural result that he thoroughly endorsed Mr.

Palmer's minute on those too candid features.   Had
he not read the phrase somewhere, " a Consummate
Actor " ?   He repeated the words to himself :   " Consummate."   He found it satisfactory.   Actor !   The
Home Secretary knew little of acting or any other
art, but he knew enough to see that this murderous
ruffian and wielder of vast economic powers, an
unscrupulous revolutionary villain for whom half
Europe was on the watch, had astonishing talent in
the wearing of a mask.

When the women had gone, the Home Secretary
drew his chair up towards his nephew-by-marriage,
the host of the evening, who had already got Mallard
at his side, and they had an interesting little conversation of three on the subject of Port.   The
Home Secretary learned all about Port in the
West Indies.   (He knew that the West Indies was
the cue.   And he could not in public show any
scepticism.)

At last (they had arranged it between themselves)
his niece's husband said, as he rose from table :

" Mr. Mallard, I think my uncle would like to say
a word to you in private upon a certain matter
before he goes up to the drawing-room.   Will you
not join us there later ? "

" Yes," put in the Home Secretary genially.

" Ah ! Exactly ! Exactly ! Are you free to give me a moment, Mr. Mallard ? "

" Certainly," answered Richard Mallard, wondering.

They moved off to the little room on the ground floor, as the other went up the stairs.

" Tell Ethel we're coming in a minute," called the Minister to his nephew as they filed away.

He saw the young fellow into the den, shut the door very cautiously behind him, and begged him to be seated, while he himself stood up and looked down upon the guest from the height of his tall, weak figure. He had always heard it said that it was an advantage to be standing up when you had to get something out to a fellow, and to have the fellow sitting down. Indeed, he remembered a passage . . . etc., etc.

" Mr. Mallard," he said abruptly. " You will allow me to call you Mallard, will you not ? "

" Eh, what ? Certainly . . . of course. That's my name. . . . What ? Certainly ! " said the bewildered young man.

" Well, yes, Mallard—we'll *take* it to be Mallard." And the Home Secretary bent down what he hoped was a searching gaze on the Consummate Actor.

" I—well—I say—why not ? " bleated Mallard.

The Home Secretary, gradually doubting the

Stand Up tradition, bethought him of another.
There was the ingratiating, the treat-him-as-an-
equal. He had read about that, too, and he seemed
to remember that it also worked wonders in drawing
out reluctant men.

He sat down, leant back in a deep leather chair,
switched off the Spiritual Current from Minatory
to Affable, and cleared his throat for the tone
customary with the great when they would show
courtesy and condescension mixed.

"Ah, Mr. Mallard," he began. "Mr. Mallard,
yes . . . Mallard. I think I heard you say during
dinner that you were from Cuba." He was putting
the Consummate Actor at his ease.

"Yes, sir," answered Mr. Mallard, very far from
being at his ease "Yes, sir, Cuba, by God, eh,
what ? "

"Ah, yes, Cuba," continued the great statesman.
Nor did his features betray the vision of West
Irania which filled him. "Well, no matter, then,
we will say Cuba. Yes, Cuba. You must
find our island climate, with its fogs and mist,
and our coal fires in summer, very trying, Mr.
Mallard."

"Not at all, sir, not at all," answered Richard
Mallard effusively. "D'you know, I can't tell you

how I like England, sir. D'you know—I've always
wanted to see England."

"Yes—ah, England," mused his superior, "England.
. . . Well, Mr. Mallard, you must remember that
it is this climate which has made us what we
are. At any rate, I can answer for it, it has made
me what I am. I well remember my dear father,
when he first took me out to Rome in the year '35—
or was it '36—no, '35—I can remember the date
exactly because it was the year of the Third
Universal Peace Congress—— " He halted abruptly.
He felt he was "running on," and he continued
abruptly :

"Well, Mr. Mallard, you'll excuse me coming to
business at once, won't you ? "

"Certainly," said Mallard yet again, marvelling
what the business might be.

"After all, it's perfectly simple, and can be put
in a very few words. Quite a few words—indeed,
ah, very few words indeed. I've always noticed
that business of any kind is much more satisfactorily
conducted when a few words are used, and when
there is no delay in getting to essentials. I recollect
when I was a baby, in the year 1925, shortly after
the Great War, you know—what a time that was !
You'd hardly believe it, Mr. Mallard, what a time

that was. I've often heard my father say he thought we should hardly pull through ! But there's something indomitable about the British character, as I remember my father saying at the time . . . "

If Mallard had dared, he would have interrupted, but he suffered the stream to flow on. And flow it did, until the ears into which it was being poured had grown dulled, as by the steady rumble of the wheels of a train. They grew alert again, however, when the harangue ended with the astounding words :

" In other words, will you not tell me frankly the extent of your powers ? "

" Eh, what ? What powers ? " gasped Mallard, with wide-open eyes.

The Home Secretary tried Finesse. He retreated.

" I presumed—tell me if I am wrong " (and he smiled wanly), " I presumed you were here to negotiate ? "

" But I don't understand," moaned Mallard.

The Home Secretary waved his hand.

" Well, at any rate, let's say for the sake of hypothesis that you are here to negotiate."

" Negotiate what ? "

" Now, now," answered the Home Secretary. " Of course, I fully appreciate your right to be reticent ; indeed, Mr. Mallard, I sympathise with it. In your position, I should adopt precisely the same attitude. But you may as well be frank with me. These things are nearly always done by third parties, as no one knows better than yourself. We are advised that you have power to open negotiations—the verbal negotiations—and all I want to know is, the extent of those powers. Then I shall know what to do and what to tell my colleagues. Have I made myself perfectly plain ? "

"Why, no," said Mallard. "Sir Henry " (he got up in his turn, in his agitation, and then plunged down again), "I am sure there must be some mistake. What ? "

The Home Secretary's face hardened—if hardened can be used of such a face at all.

"We have not very much time on this occasion, Mr. Mallard," he remarked. "We must be going upstairs immediately."

Mallard broke in with a most moving appeal :

"Look here, Sir Henry," he begged. "D'you know, I simply don't understand at all about this. There's some mistake. My name is Mallard—just Mallard. What ? " (The Home Secretary nodded, with a vast appearance of omniscience.) "I am travelling in Europe, that's all. I'm very much honoured, you know, by these attentions, and oh, I don't know—all this from new acquaintances—what? But what is it you want? No, I'm afraid that sounds rude . . . I mean, what about it all, you know?"

He was startled by the unexpected clarity of the reply. The Home Secretary pulled out his watch and said:

"Mr. Mallard, to cut a long story short, what about that Concession? I take it you have approached no one?"

"Concession, sir," said Richard Mallard, opening wide eyes. "Concession? I mean to say, you know, I don't quite understand."

"Well, Mr. Mallard," went on the Home Secretary suavely, "of course, there must be no question of negotiation with anyone but ourselves. That's the first point. I take it that is understood?"

Young Mr. Mallard nodded, with eyes still wider open, understanding still less than ever, but thinking it courteous to jerk the chin.

"For which," continued the Secretary of State, "there would of course be a consideration; or shall we say an equivalent?"

"Oh, yes, of course, of course," said Mallard. "Yes, naturally."

"Now, Mr. Mallard," went on the other, glancing

8

*Concealed Genius of the Home Secretary in his
interrogation of that Consummate Actor
Richard Mallard*

*Concealed Genius of that Consummate Actor Richard
Mallard under the interrogation of the
Home Secretary*

again at his watch, " I think we may as well have it in plain terms. You are prepared to deal with us now, and with us only. In fact, I do not want to put it too bluntly, but you understand that if the necessity arose we could *compel*."

" Eh, what ? " said the startled Mallard.

" The Government has full powers to deal with any untoward propositions from private individuals, and I may assure you, Mr. Mallard, that the Government will exercise it ruthlessly. Ruth-er-less-ly," he repeated with mild vigour, tapping vaguely upon the upholstered arm of the chair.

Richard Mallard was getting frightened. He planted both elbows on the little table at which he sat, making his coffee cup rattle with the sharpness of the gesture, and put up a bewildered face between his hands towards the wielder of such thunderbolts.

" I don't understand, sir," he said. " Damned if I do ! I beg your pardon, I mean. . . . But you know, really, what's it all about ? "

The Home Secretary sighed. He rose dispiritedly and with the difficulty of age from his low chair, shaking his head.

" I am afraid, Mr. Mallard," he said, " that we shall get no forwarder."

" Oh, sir, I beg of you," interjected the unfortunate youth . . .

" No, no, Mr. Mallard. We have kept the others
waiting too long. We must join them upstairs.
I had certainly hoped " (shaking his head) " that we
might at least have opened the negotiation this
evening. But as you persist . . ."

" Upon my honour," protested the unfortunate
young man, " I do assure you . . . what ? . . ."

" It must be for another time, sir," quavered his
senior ; and he led the way painfully upstairs,
muttering a reminiscence of similar difficulties
encountered by our representative at Delhi during
the great Indian Emancipation affair all those
years ago.

*   *   *   *

It was not for nothing that the Prime Minister
was called efficient, or even by some a godsend—
especially after the terrible experience of the country
under Lady Sarah Palasch. The niece's butler,
honourably discharging a duty for which he had been
amply paid, had rung up the moment the Home
Secretary and his unfortunate victim had gone
upstairs, and within five minutes the Home Secretary
himself was summoned to the telephone.

"Well?" said the determined contralto voice.

"He won't say anything. Not a word."

There was a pause.

"He must be *made* to," answered the contralto voice firmly.

"*I* can't make him," quavered the reply.

"I didn't think you could." (A pause.) "I shall know what to do when I've thought over it. Meanwhile see they keep an eye on him till I've decided. *You* needn't touch it again." Her quick ear caught a profound sigh of relief from the other end of the wire. "Oh, yes," she added, with a touch of temper in the contralto voice, "it gives *you* a rest, I know! But damn it all, man! what are you there for? . . . However, it's no good pestering you. I'll decide what to do—later."

She rang off.

Hardly was this happy release effected, and the sufferer half-way up the stairs again, with a load off his mind, when he was respectfully summoned back to the telephone again. The Prime Minister had had an after-thought, and the wires were at work.

"Look here, Harry," said the Contralto Voice, "there's something I forgot: Of course, you would have thought of it; but still, I ought to say it at the first opportunity. You understand that there's to be no arrest. Only watch him. If we have to arrest, that will come after, perhaps, but we must get all we can out of him first."   ·

"Yes, yes, of course, Mary. Oh, I understood that from the first. It's common sense, isn't it? I very well remember during the last administration . . ."

The Contralto Voice was standing no nonsense.

"Look here, I can't stop here talking all night. You'll give orders that there's to be no arrest?"

"Yes," said the Minister. "We've got the plain clothes men watching him, of course. But they won't do anything without reporting."

"All right," said the Contralto. "Good night."

*   *   *   *

No, the Plain Clothes Men would do nothing without reporting. If there is one police system in the world which really works well, it is that of our beloved country. The Plain Clothes Men would do nothing before they had reported. But was it equally certain that nothing would be done to them? That was the little snag in the scheme which neither the head of the Home Office nor the far more capable head of the State had sufficiently considered.

CHAPTER V

THE Home Secretary went upstairs again to the drawing-room, full of gloom. He found Mallard very uncomfortable and hardly knowing what to say or do : the niece and her husband trying in their turn to put him at his ease and failing damnably.

At last the niece, with the exquisite tact of that rich world, turned him out. She made it clear that he should go, and he, poor devil, was too glad of the chance to mind the contrast between the manners of London and those of Havana.

It is to Sir Henry Hardham's credit that he saw Mallard down to the door and into a taxi there waiting : nor was it mentioned that the taxi had been there, waiting, for half an hour, and that the taxpayer would meet the cost.

Just on getting in Mallard had noticed a short, sturdy-looking man (who seemed to have been dining somewhere in the neighbourhood, for he also was in evening dress) get into another taxi fifty yards behind him up the street.

The thing was of no importance ; it was but a casual glance at one out of a hundred such sights at that hour. But the man's face was full in the light of the electric lamp, and was noticeable enough. After a moment the harassed Mallard forgot all about it. He gave the direction of his hotel, stepped in, and sank back morally exhausted.

That short drive south and eastwards from Mayfair was not as short as it might have been, and perhaps someone more suspicious or with more knowledge of the world than this poor young rich man might have been intrigued when, to begin with, the taxi pulled up short at the corner of Mount Street. The driver laboriously got off the seat, taking plenty of time over it, put his head in at the window, and said he had quite forgotten the address to which he had to go. He might have been still more intrigued when, five hundred yards on, the vehicle stopped with a grinding noise, and the driver, jumping off once more, assured him that he would not be a moment, and began hitting things with some iron instrument or other. At last he was delivered safe and sound. But the journey had taken seven minutes more than it ought to have done.

He was not in the best of tempers, therefore, as

he paid the man off and went through the revolving door ; and there, comfortably sprawling in a deep chair in the lounge, smoking a cigar, and in a seeming indifference of bliss to the world about him, was, most unmistakably, the gentleman who had taken that other taxi. He had apparently got to the hotel first. It was a coincidence, no more ; but the victim was in a jerky mood. He steadied himself. Perhaps he was exaggerating that coin- cidence a little, eh ? But his mind still turned upon the sturdy one. Moreover, he could not get it out of his head that the short and sturdy one had watched him over his shoulder as he went off out of the lounge towards the lift.

Richard Mallard that night at first slept ill. It may well have been the bad wine at the niece's ; but it was also a confused dread of a situation of which he could make nothing, but which he felt vaguely to be a menace. What on earth was it all about ? he thought, as he lay staring at the darkness. Why on earth should he, a blameless young man, whose only trouble was that he had so few acquaintances and whose chief desire was to see the world, suddenly find himself a guest in these great houses and the subject of mysterious cross-examinations ?

Then suddenly it flashed upon him! It must have something to do—it *could* only have something to do—with that which he had always been told was but a wild myth of his poor old predecessor. It was the Piræus Concession. Still, he was astonished that the politicians (he begged their pardons—Statesmen) should think it so important.

Yes, that was it. That explained the mysterious attitude of Sir Henry. And he began to blame himself for his stupidity in not having discovered it at the time. But it certainly was astounding. He was growing sleepy. . . . But he had found some solution of the problem, however wild and unlikely, and to find it relaxed the strain. He slept well till morning.

* * * *

Mr. Chinny, a Plain Clothes Man, hadn't an ounce of burden on his mind. You may think that odd in a man of such a profession, but I assure you it is so. Power, that chief corrupting devil in the ruin of men's souls, had never come near him. I blush to say that he received less than Eight Pounds a week. It was his simple duty to Keep an Eye on Them.

Not his to ask why They were being Kept an

Eye On. He might surmise, for his private amusement, like a man doing a crossword puzzle, whether They on whom he Kept that Eye were criminals, politicians, bankers, lunatics, or counter agents; but it was not his to go further than to surmise.

I do not know whether any reader of this charming story has ever been a Plain Clothes Man himself (or a plain clothes woman herself—which God Forbid! for women go on their clothes), but I can assure those who are ignorant of the profession that one of its chief charms is the enormous variety of the experience. Now you are a bargee, now a miner, now a Tommy, now an omnibus conductor: and then again—and that is the happy moment— a Toff.

When the Toff Stunt is on the Plain Clothes Man is like a schoolboy on holiday. Not only has he an ample allowance, but he can spend it like water. I am told that they do not even ask for accounts!

Not every Plain Clothes Man can do the Toff lay. There must be a passable accent at least, and an ability to walk in pumps, or even in boots, without appearing to stamp out the embers of rebellion or cause the floors of palaces to shake beneath your

tread. Yet does not that great Department of
State of which the Plain Clothes Man is a humble
member demand for its occasional Toff gags any
family connection, nor even any instruction. A
quiet, pleasant voice, a reasonable tone, and
something of the actor which no Plain Clothes Man
can do without, are all that is required.

Mr. Chinny was on a Toff Stunt. He was on the
Toff Stunt at the Titanic Hotel and in clover. He
was on the Toff Stunt as "covering" Richard
Mallard.

He had noticed the casual glance thrown at him
as Mallard came in the night before. He noticed a
more troubled look at the fifth time of crossing.

The worthy young man upon whom he had been
told to Keep his Eye was taking notice, and that
would never do. He had marked the rather
suspicious stare which the said young man had given
him when they had crossed for the tenth time, and
he was beginning to think that the observer was
himself observed. He must be wary.

Yes, he had noticed these things, but they had
not yet much disturbed him. It was his business
to Keep an Eye, and he was not going to be bothered.
If you ask me why the Department is so unintelligent
in its choice of men, I cannot tell you. I suppose

because it is a peculiar and complicated department in these happy, democratic days of ours, when so large a proportion of the population is occupied in spying upon the other part.

Richard Mallard was not English; he was, to use an old-fashioned term, Colonial—he was of the New World. Therefore he did not breakfast in his bedroom, still less in bed. He came down like an honest man to breakfast in the gilded halls of the Titanic Hotel. He did not know that while he had been dressing a page had warned Mr. Chinny both of his descent and of the table he was to occupy for breakfast.

But he was fully aware of Mr. Chinny when he came down, for Mr. Chinny was at the very next table : with his back not quite turned ; a three-quarter view.

And Mr. Chinny was in glory—almost in beatitude. It is one of the splendours of the Toff Service that among the perquisites are good clothes, and you have a right to keep them. None of your reach-me-downs : you are measured for them, and you acquire a wardrobe which in due course your wife sells or retains for grand occasions, according to the finances of the household.

I am bad at describing clothes, but I can tell

you generally that Mr. Chinny was in a sort of grey
which had no small cousinship with purple ; and
his tie suggested at once the Guards and Balliol,
though not a replica of either of those symbols ;
that he had gilt links ; that he had spats. But,
on the top of having all these things, he also had
discretion. The make-up was not exaggerated, the
covering of his carcass was that of the well-to-do
English gentleman—only an inch or two on the
bounder side, for he had taken for his Model the
Secretary of State for the Fine Arts, as being a
Lord.

Richard Mallard ate his breakfast in some gloom,
which the newspaper he was reading, being conducted
by a Peer and therefore all murders and gallows,
did not relieve. His meal over, he strolled towards
the big lounge, and was at last quite seriously
annoyed to notice that Mr. Chinny was also strolling,
at about the same pace, half a corridor's length
behind him. As a piece of synchrony it was
excellent ; as a piece of deception it was bad.
And once again, if you ask me why they use such
men in that Department, I make the same reply.
When things get too large and too complicated they
usually get rather badly run.

Anyhow, Mr. Chinny was happy — so far.   He

Inexperience of Mr. Mallard on the operations of our old and complex Society

liked the atmosphere of luxury, the pages in buttons
bawling numbers at the tops of their voices, the
footmen in powdered hair, the gilded columns, the
complicated food with foreign names (even at
breakfast), the insolence of the waiters—all that
suited him. He did not get nearly enough of it.
Perhaps not twice in a twelvemonth. It made
him feel like a hero in a cinema when he did get it,
and he had not had it since he was shadowing that
Crook from the Argentine just over a year before.
Indeed, the choice of Mr. Chinny was due (it is
the way with some organisations) to luck. The
Crook had been nabbed through missing his train
by over-sleeping. He had been arrested in his
bedroom, and Mr. Chinny, with real genius, had
suddenly bethought him to say that the drowsiness
was due to a drug administered by him in the
foreigner's coffee the night before. Nor did his
superiors notice that the day happened to be that
in which winter time changes to summer time.

To this accident was due Mr. Chinny's high
employment on this occasion, and of such is the
Kingdom of Heaven.

But in the eyes of Heaven, if not in his own,
Mr. Chinny, in spite of his reputation with the
Department, was not of a calibre for his task.

9

Mallard, already exasperated, was beginning to be sure that the man was shadowing him. The lift delivered him to his room ten minutes later, and behold—even as he was unlocking the door, the key of which had stuck for a moment, a second journey of the elevator delivered Mr. Chinny, who walked with nonchalance towards a neighbouring door. It speaks whole libraries for the ineptitude of Mr. Chinny that it could goad such a youth as Richard Mallard ; but Richard Mallard was getting really annoyed.

Mr. Chinny did not stay long in that upper room. He knew his stupid mechanical instructions far too well for that. His place lay at the strategic points of the exits. Early as was the hour, he ordered a drink, and sprawled back sipping it in a wicker-chair of the lounge, waiting for his patient to appear. The Usual Informant came and told him that Richard Mallard had rung and might be down at any moment ; therefore did Mr. Chinny go out for a moment to speak to the Other Gentleman, he who was entrusted with the task of Eye Keeping for the Exterior Department, or, as we call it in the Profession, the Street Side.

This other gentleman, Mr. Corbould by name, but the name is of no great importance, we shall not have much more to do with it (or him), was a very solemn sort of gentleman, disarming suspicion by his lugubrious features. He might have been a Mute out of work—save, again, as in the case of his colleague, for his clothes.

For Mr. Corbould's clothes were much more subtle than Mr. Chinny's. They suited the part most exactly. They were the clothes of the solid, unpretentious middle class: a literary man, you would have said, making under £1,000 a year, but with leisure enough to stroll up and down the streets observing mankind. They were of a dark grey, with a double-breasted coat. He wore no spats, his boots were uncompromising, his bowler was clean, but no more *chic* than Hungerford Bridge; and his tie was a plain black. Scholars—and I do not pretend to be one—have decided that Mr. Corbould was dressed from top to toe by a great Expert of the Department; whereas Mr. Chinny chose his clothes himself. For Mr. Corbould was not married; his clothes were not a perquisite; they had to be worn until they looked old, and then regularly returned to the Department—where I suppose they become a perquisite of some other equally intelligent and devoted servant of our admired political system.

Increasing apprehension of Mr. Mallard on the operations of our old and complex Society

Anyhow, thus was Mr. Corbould habited, when Mr. Chinny entered into conversation with him under the simple form of telling him to keep his weather eye peeled.

Even as they were speaking, Richard Mallard strode up and shot a vicious glance at them before he went by up the street. Not five minutes later, he looked back over his shoulder ; he was at boiling point. There, unmistakably, were the two men ; one whom he had not seen before, and the other the detestable sturdy one. Mild as he was, he was getting fed right up. He turned round and challenged.

" I don't know your motive, you know, in following me about like this," he said, " but I resent it, and I mean to say I won't have it . . . what ? "

" 'Oo's follering of yer ? " said the lugubrious literary Corbould.

" I beg your pardon. I think you are under some misapprehension," winningly insinuated the more instructed Chinny.

Richard Mallard was young, he was unused to our complex old civilisation, and his blood was up.

" Look here," he said. " I give you fair warning— eh ? I'm going about my affairs, you know—what ?

and if I see either of your damned mugs about, let alone both of them . . . "

Mr. Chinny smiled as charmingly as his round face would permit, and by an unseen motion of the forefinger to Mr. Corbould indicated that he would do well to keep his potato trap shut and not give the show away.

" My dear sir," he said again, " I do assure you that you are under a misapprehension. Speaking as one gentleman to another, I tender you full compensation for disturbance." Whereat he raised his hat (not knowing how to take it off). The less alert Corbould was late in the gesture, and a moment after they had turned aside.

Two or three times that morning Richard Mallard, as he went about taking in the sights of London on that summer's day, looked hesitatingly over his shoulder to make sure of his privacy. He saw no sign that he was pursued.

He was glad he had spoken as he had. It made him feel manly. It made him feel that he had won a battle. After all, one only had to put one's foot down, and it was all right, what ? But why the devil should he be victimised like this, eh ? I mean to say, What had he done ? What was it all about ? Poor old William Mallard's mania was all very well, but why should it lead to this? Curse it, you know!

He was free. That noble edifice, the National Gallery, standing over what has been strangely called the finest site in Europe, attracted his wandering steps. He knew it was full of pictures, and pictures are something to look at, anyhow. In he went. And after half an hour out he came.

Now whereas your Londoner or even your Englishman born comes down the steps briskly into Trafalgar Square again when he has fulfilled the desire of his soul with the glories of Art, Richard Mallard, delighting in the prospect of a new city, leaned over the high balustrade and surveyed the passers-by. He mused over the vast crowds streaming past the southern side of Trafalgar Square; then suddenly—his eyes were young and good—he did most unmistakably perceive two gentlemen peeping cautiously round the plinth of that pillar which supports the sailor whose name is one with England; the first Lord Nelson. To be quite accurate, when I say the plinth, I mean Landseer's south-eastern lion, for under the lee of that noble beast had Mr. Chinny and Mr. Corbould been waiting in no little boredom since the moment when they had spied their chase entering the square acres of canvas.

They had observed all the rules that are set down in the little secret books, and still better exemplified in the occasional lectures delivered to the Force by its Instructors. They had seen without being seen. But when the quarry had come out of the majestic portals, his unusual action in delaying at the balustrade to survey the life of London had thrown them a little out of gear. He had not come down the steps; he might have gone back. They were a little anxious. Hence that timid peep; and hence the discovery not of him by them, but of them by him.

"Strike me!" said the literary figure in the quiet dark grey double-breasted coat.

"Curse me!" said the well-to-do gentleman in the lighter grey which had purple haunting its shadows.

"'E must've gorn one way or the other; 'e carn't 'ave vanished!" said the first.

"There he is!" suddenly struck in the other, in an excited murmur, and they both ducked.

But it was too late. Meekness was roused to Wrath, and there was Anger in the Humble as the Psalmist has it. Richard Mallard had crossed the northern street at top speed under the very nose of George Washington; he was running down the

steps ; he was striding across the open space by
the fountains, with strange and new determination
in his eye. Mr. Chinny and Mr. Corbould observed
his movements with the utmost discretion, a mere
corner of their faces squinting round the edge of the
great stones that hid them, and straining their
necks in that prawn-like attitude to which their
confraternity are trained—so that the eye alone
protrudes and nothing of the body to which it
belongs can be perceived.

But Richard Mallard was not to be baulked. He
had seen ; and he had made no mistake. They
were hiding under the shadow of the lion, and he
would not have it. He'd be damned if he'd stand
it ! What ?

He carried in his right hand one of those formidable
canes which are regarded in the New World as
necessary to European travel. On his features was
a still more formidable determination. He strode
round the plinth, and faced them—just as the Twin
Brethren were covering their tracks by pointing out
to each other with great excitement two pigeons
circling in the air above.

"Now then, you know, damn you!" shouted Mallard.

They looked round—startled, as well they might
be, to hear that angry voice from so mild a man ;

*Breakdown of Mr. Mallard's efforts to comprehend
our old and complex Society*

but they were much more startled when the stout
cane fell upon them both impartially, belabouring
them with a violence which spoke worlds for Richard
Mallard's novel choler and nothing at all for his
discretion. And in less than two two's he was in
the hands of four uniformed giants, three of whom
were holding his arms and legs, one his collar with
the right hand, while with the other he put a whistle
to his lips to summon aid.

If Richard Mallard had desired to investigate by
personal experiment the character and quality of
London police drill, he could not have had a better
opportunity. It seemed to him that he had had
no idea until that moment of how strong human
muscles can be, or with what beautiful unity trained
men can act. To the artistic eye of one onlooker
at least, an aged Italian officer who had taken to
coaching in his native tongue for a livelihood, it
was one of the most delightful examples of military
precision conceivable. He made a sketch of it,
which hangs in my rooms to this day, and which I
have often had occasion to admire.

The crowd which gathered round did not impede
the majestic march to justice, and Richard Mallard
within a quarter of an hour was undergoing that
fate which all honest and impulsive men must suffer

in what the present Lord Winklebeach himself has called " our highly complex urban organisation." It was a very small, very clean cell, at the little lattice in the door of which a maleficent and threatening eye from time to time appeared.

*　　*　　*　　*

All details had gone down in the book ; torture had been spared ; he had capitulated. There was the name Richard Mallard, the address of the hotel, and all the rest of it. He had admitted the loud complaint of the double-breasted one and the spatted one, who, I need hardly say, still kept up their character of plain citizens (not plain-clothes citizens) before their uniformed colleagues—one of whom, I am sorry to admit, winked enormously at them both with his other eye.

One thing Richard Mallard did do out of the ordinary, and it was what men nearly always do under these circumstances, when they have the luck to be able to do it at all. He told them the truth about himself. He said that he was a tourist, with no friends in England. He told the truth about his motive, that he was sure he had been followed by these people, that he did not know why he was thus annoyed, and that he had been moved to intolerable anger by such insolence ; but he added :

" If you doubt my word, or wish to know who I am, I was dining last night at Lady Corvan's. The Home Secretary was there, I was introduced to him, he had already heard of me, and I think he would answer for me."

The policeman who was rapidly entering all these things in a book did so most dispassionately. He doubted the statement ; he had heard that sort of thing before. On the other hand, one must run no risks. And therefore, while Richard Mallard was duly locked in and occupying his mind as best he could, the telephone was at work again, and messages were being sent out.

Wild horses shall not tear from me the details of what followed : but I will tell you this much—that there was the usual muddle, when it is important for the Executor and the Judiciary to communicate. Servants got the wrong message, masters and mistresses were out, hurried secretaries sent notes to houses from which their chiefs were absent ; first and last about a score of human beings up and down political London were occupied in one tangle after another. Thus it was that Richard Mallard spent the night in the cells, and it was not until a quarter past eight o'clock the next morning that the Home Office had got the thing in black and white ; Sir Henry Hardham might, after Palaver, have acted by ten—but before twenty minutes past eight that early-rising matron, the Prime Minister, had received the S.O.S.—and acted on it.

The Court opened, and Mr. Service, the highly respected stipendiary magistrate, was in his most judicial mood. It was impressive to watch the deep lines on that impassive face, instinct with order, a very mask of Justice.

The two injured gentlemen gave their evidence in plain, straightforward fashion, to which the dread occupant of the tribunal listened with unchanging features, as though carved in teak.

He heard their tale : how they were Members of the Force in plain clothes employed to watch the defendant, how they had in no way molested him, when they were suddenly subjected to this violent assault. The uniformed men corroborated the story. Richard Mallard could only give his version, and admit there was no excuse for his action. But this perpetual annoyance of being followed and watched wherever he went had got the better of him, and he had had the imprudence to strike them.

*Powerful Impartiality of Mr. Stipendiary Service
while hearing evidence*

Then it was, when all had been heard—without the aid of counsel, in the simplest fashion—that the zealous servants of public order got the shock of their lives.

Mr. Service rose to the full measure of his high office. His features assumed such a force of concentrated energy as made the boldest tremble. In stern and dreadful tones he declared that a more outrageous abuse of a private citizen by the police had never before come to his notice. His voice rose in grand organ tones as he warmed to his subject, so that those few in Court who had some acquaintance with the artistic side of Justice lamented once again that sad, forgotten episode in the magistrate's earlier career which had precluded him from occupying a place among the greater Judges. His indignation was magnificent.

He insisted that this kind of thing was getting far too frequent. What had astonished him most—and (he would add) saddened and disgusted him—was the conduct of the aggrieved parties, so-called. Yes, he used the word " so-called." Did they think he was without experience of the actions of the police, or without means of judging those limits which should never be exceeded in the prosecution of their duties ? It was an outrageous thing, he

Stern denunciation by Mr. Service of the Police for interfering with the Liberty of the Subject

thundered, that honest men could no longer pursue their peaceable avocations without molestation of this kind. The prosecution had themselves admitted that they knew nothing against their victim ; they had merely obeyed orders. But that was not enough ; who had given those orders ? And by what right ?

Really, to hear Mr. Service, you would have said that Divine Vengeance was revealing itself, and that the Immemorial Liberties of Englishmen had found a more than human champion.

But as for the official side, to compare their feelings to those of a man who has suddenly received a blow on the last button of his waistcoat would give but a pale image of their consternation. For them, it was as though the world had come to an end. Who was safe ?

The thing was soon over. Mr. Service was at the pains of delivering a terse peroration directly addressed to the prisoner, whom he treated with deference as a sort of public hero.

" You have gallantly admitted that you were to blame in acting upon impulse. Though I understand that you were not born in this country, you have yet shown what an inheritance of English blood can do. You have frankly admitted your fault, but you have, as you were richly entitled to do, emphasised the intolerable provocation by which you were goaded. I will not even inflict a nominal fine ; but I shall take care that the gross assault which has amply been proved against your aggressors shall be forwarded to the proper quarter."

There was slight applause in Court, which for a wonder was not suppressed.

The Press and its politicians were very well tuned on this little business. One of the Back-Benchers wanted to make a stunt of it, and threatened and grumbled a good deal when pressure was put upon him to use the soft pedal ; *The Times* very dutifully scrapped its third leader ; the *Spectator* only had one note, of a moderate sort, pointing out that these methods of secret police were happily unknown in England, and hoping that what looked like the beginnings of a vile continental system would not be heard of again. There was just sufficient emphasis to prevent the Department from reacting, but not so much as to bring Mallard into the limelight ; a relief for which he was profoundly grateful—but for which the Prime Minister was more grateful still. Seeing how many of these things had been bungled, it was a feather in her cap, or rather in the cap of her secretariat, that it had been so well managed :

and they were not slow in letting the hero **of the** business know how he had been befriended in high quarters.

The first move came in the shape of a very nice little note brought to the Titanic by hand, from William Delavere, one of the more private of the private Private Secretaries. It told Mr. Mallard how strongly the authorities had felt for him during the ordeal to which he had been subjected, and asked very politely for an interview at any time which suited him. Would he come to Downing Street, or would he prefer that Mr. Delavere should come to his hotel? Any day, place or hour that was convenient to him would be convenient to Mr. Delavere. There never was such smoothness!

Poor Mallard! He had not desired it. All **he** wanted was to be left alone—and here was **this** mysterious machine at work again!

However, it was an honour; it came from very near the Throne. He sent an answer by the messenger saying he would be free that very day at noon, and as for the place, why, he would be obliged if Mr. Delavere would make it the Cousin's Club, to which he had been very kindly admitted **as** an honorary guest by the efforts of his travelling acquaintance, Mr. Palmer. It was a good, respectable

club, not so grand as to overawe the stranger,
full of Civil Servants and with a sprinkling of
politicians, a few sailors, and one or two writers ;
and the rest, nonentities of leisure. Could they
meet there at noon ?

Mr. Delavere would be delighted.

Therefore was it that just after 11 o'clock that
day the Prime Minister, with that Napoleonic touch
for which she was already famous, was plotting
out the main lines of the staff work with her
subordinate ; or rather, giving orders.

" The chances are you'll get nothing out of him,
Billy. Old Harry couldn't get a word out of
him at his niece's last night. Of course, Harry's a
fool, but still the man seems deep enough for
anything. He acts the Boob to the *life !* . . . so
they say."

" I'll do my best," answered Delavere modestly.

" Well, mind you, I don't expect miracles. And
if he keeps dumb I shan't blame you. I expect it ;
and if he goes on being dumb too long—why, *then*
you know . . . " and she made the gesture of turning
a key in a lock.

Determined was her eye as she did it. She would
have made a most efficient Warder.

" Yes ! Yes ! . . . But it hasn't come to that

yet," cried Delavere, " and if I *do* make him speak, what's my orders ? "

" Why, then the whole thing turns upon the form the little courtesy on our part shall take." And once more did Mary Bullar indulge in gesture : this time the passing of imaginary coins between the thumb and forefinger.

" A counter-concession is the best form, isn't it ? " suggested Delavere. " That's what they did in the Dagon business. When he'd got the concession of the navigation for our people we gave his bank at Budapest the floating of the Forestry thing-um-bob."

" Have you found out with what companies he is connected ? "

" Not yet," answered the secretary. " He might not be overtly connected with any. Under the Annihilationist system, as you know, private corporations are not permitted. We shall probably find he's got most of his own private boodle in British Funds. These Asiatics know where to keep it. I shall have to find out who are the go-betweens before I can know what interest he has in any Company or Bank of ours, or in any Continental or American group."

The Prime Minister thought for a moment, tapping

her false teeth with the nail of her forefinger, in a gesture at once ladylike and characteristic.

"It doesn't matter," she said at last. "He can always make a new company if he likes, or we could make one for him. And then we could give it the counter-concession . . . for instance, something in the new East African oil-field."

"Suppose he prefers a national loan for West Irania?" suggested Delavere.

"Well," patiently replied his chief, "if he prefers a loan he can have it. I arranged that with the banks and Douglas the moment I heard the fellow was sailing from New York. He would get his commission on the loan, and that might give us more of a hold over him. Have you heard whether he's putting his price high?"

"I've heard nothing," said Delavere. "Of course, sometimes one finds with these new Asiatic establishments that there are points on which they are not allowed to yield. Moscow won't let them."

"Yes," said the Prime Minister. "That's the worst of it. At least, it's the worse for us, but of course it's very convenient for them. Moscow calls them independent one day, and treats them as dependent the next, according as it suits their book —it's the same all over the Asiatic Confederation."

" That's it," said Delavere.

" Well, do your best. Remember he wants us to keep up the question of Cuba, and all that. Humour him. Don't stay to luncheon with him. Come back here, and we'll lunch together and you can tell me what's happened."

So the young man was dismissed to the congenial task of one more negotiation—and if he did well in it, that meant a big step upward for *him*.

He found Mr. Mallard waiting for him in a highly nervous mood—or at least the outward and well acted appearance of such. His whole appearance was a shock to Delavere. He'd been warned, to be sure, but if it *was* acting it was superb : the gentle, worried eye, the uncertain mouth, the radiant innocence.

Anyhow, he must play up to the side : his *vis-à-vis* was registering tremors. Delavere therefore made it his first business to soothe.

He shook hands in a sort of brotherly manner, as though he had come to see Mallard for Mallard's sake. He talked of his journey from the United States (without a word of West Irania). He talked at length and with emphasis about the great annoyance which he must have suffered, and how much everybody regretted it. He even hinted vaguely at compensation—but he did not carry that vein too far, for fear of spoiling the coming effect of great sums by the mention of smaller ones. He led the conversation round very gradually, and in the most general terms, to matters of territory, of international relations, of the establishment of boundaries, to a concession—all of which was bewildering Greek to his victim.

And then he put his hand suddenly upon the centre of the affair : saying, almost abruptly :

"Now, Mr. Mallard, you can guess what I have come for. You will see the Prime Minister yourself later, I hope ; but I want to be able to tell her more or less the lines upon which you will proceed."

"Yes," said Mallard. "Lines about what ? "

"I thought as much ! " was the phrase that rose secretly within Delavere's mind. But outwardly he smiled as he said :

"Why, how much should be included."

"Eh, what ? You mean, what area ? " said Mallard.

"Yes, of course."

"Why, d'you know, if anything final is decided, I don't see why the whole of it shouldn't be included, eh ! What ? " answered the young man simply. "So far as *I've* anything to say. What ? But, you know, I don't think there's much in it."

"Oh! Come!" said Delavere, beaming.

"I don't, you know, honestly . . . I don't want to rob you, what?"

"Yes, of course," Delavere waved his hand. "Of course. But we can arrive at some idea of the thing to begin with." He mastered his face well. It wore no more than a look of mild appreciation. But, within, young Delavere's soul was beatified. He had succeeded where that old ass Hardham had failed! The Envoy was beginning to talk! Talk! And he, Delavere, had worked it. He saw new talents appearing. He was heading for great things. He was already in imagination a governor at the least—or better, an ambassador.

"Well, but you know," began Mallard, almost stammering in his embarrassment, "you know, honestly, I don't think it's worth *anything*."

Really this was coming it strong! But Delavere wasn't going to be baulked. He'd open the oyster, and he would eat it.

"It's a little delicate," he began, hesitating. "But these matters have to be gone into some time . . . and I was going, before we talked of terms, to ask whether you, personally, might not be willing to consider . . ."

Mallard was quite open.

" Well, I'd have to send over for the facts first
and get all details from over there, don't you know.
They've got them over there."

" Oh, don't bother about them just now," said
Delavere, with the utmost geniality and in his most
reassuring tones. " You surely can give us a general
idea—just a general idea. We can go into details
later. And first of all—— " he coughed. " It's a
little delicate as I said, but *may* I suggest . . . "

" Yes, eh ! What ? " contributed Mallard usefully,
staring like a pair of saucers.

" Well, to put it plainly, I was going to suggest
that we might consider giving you . . . "

" But I'm sure that wouldn't be honest ! Eh ? "
very candidly advanced the honest Mallard. " I
can't take money for a thing not, what-you-may-
call-it, you know, decided, eh ? What ? "

" We'll see to that," said Delavere, more genially
still. He had made up his mind to call a halt at
that stage and pick up the threads later when he
had seen his chief.

" I'm really extremely glad," he added, " that
we have been able to understand each other so
easily."

With that he firmly drove the conversation down
another street, got it on to the interesting matter

of a debate which was to take place in the House next day, would Mr. Mallard like a good seat under the Gallery. No, Mr. Mallard was much obliged, but he had other plans. And so he had! He was for the Lakes. But he kept it dark.

Well, Mr. Delavere hoped they might soon meet again, and so made for the door and his taxi in something as near jubilation as an astute young man of the world ever gets.

Mallard left for his hotel and swept the lounge with his eye for a Detective. It was empty, save for uniforms—and even these he suspected. He went up to his room looking behind him two or three times on the way, and locked himself in. There he held his head in his hands and suffered agonies of fear and incomprehension combined. He was tangled béyond the limits of entanglement. How *could* you promise something you hadn't yet got? You might pledge yourself verbally, but when it came to documents? Eh? What? And what on earth had the "Mallard Millions" and Piræus to do with the British Government?

Perhaps, he surmised (for he was innocent of these things), there was some bargain on with the authorities in Texas; perhaps they wanted to have no chance, however remote, of complications, and so

would pay him to clear out of the road. But would
it be honest ? And (again) why the British ?

Anyhow, he was beginning to feel important.
And no wonder. But he was also beginning to be
thoroughly frightened. He wasn't made for that
sort of thing, you know. He didn't like it. What
puzzled him most was that he had not heard a word
or a hint of all this before sailing. No one at home
had the least inkling of it. To the very moment
when he left, old William Mallard's mania was
still a laughing-stock and the rents of Piræus were
being duly paid to those who had been in possession
for half a life-time. Why all this mystery now ? . . .
and then being followed and that ghastly night in
the cells, and all the fog and worry of it—oh ! Lord !
He started at his own thoughts. He thought he
heard a sound outside. He unbolted the door
suddenly, to catch the fellow at the keyhole. There
was no one there.

Then hunger did what terror could not do, and this
young man went down to lunch in the grill-room,
where every one of a hundred eaters, black, white,
and levantine, was for him an enemy and a spy.

*   *   *   *

And in Downing Street Mr. Delavere had reported
and Mrs. Bullar had thoughtfully frowned.

"Oh! He's playing that stale old trick, is he?" she said. "Referring to the Other Partner?"

"Yes, but he's talking at last," answered Delavere, a little crestfallen. "That's something!"

"Yes," admitted Mary Bullar, "that's something. Humph!"

CHAPTER VI

ON the morning after Richard Mallard had enjoyed his little adventure with the police, both veiled and open, in the very hour of his handsome acquittal, Lord Delisport, empire maker, newspaper owner and Marquis, was walking up and down his office, deeply engaged in thought. It is a habit grown too rare in men of his exalted world; but when I tell you that he was thinking about money, you will understand both him and me the better.

He stopped in his pacing and stood with his hands in his pockets, slightly bent forward and looking at the blank wall before him as though it were some commercial rival against whom he had most honourably to pit his mammoth brain.

He might have stood for a statue in the older fashion—a symbolic statue, detailed and living—of the lordly intellects which direct big business.

The strong, anchored will stamped deep upon features rather puissant than refined, the restrained but sharply - directed glance of the eyes, their prominence, their slightly yellowish hue, these and the multiple contours of the lower face and chin, were sufficient to mark his genius.

Friends in the City had nicknamed him the Toad ; the kindly and humorous epithet expressed but half a truth, for his expression bore none of that gaping innocence which is so characteristic of Batrachians. But it is true that he was cool and that the surface of his soul was unguent, while his portraits—especially those in full face—did sometimes startlingly suggest the humble animal whom he thus honoured.

Lord Delisport was a man in whom the Captain of Industry could be discovered at a glance. Short, clumsy, bald, save for a thick fringe of curling brown hair round the base of his head, with a short thick nose, a rapid walk, in spite of a considerable girth, and a trick of exclaiming, " Wot say ? " when he would gather your meaning, all marked the modern commercial master and English Peer.

No one need wonder at his millions. Such men command millions of right ; the wonder rather is that he had remained at a weekly wage of under four pounds until so late an age as thirty-seven, and that his first piece of good fortune had lifted him into the rank of millionaires before his fiftieth year.

George Goodge, first Marquis of Delisport

Lord Delisport always thought more clearly when he had jotted down the headings of his subject.

He had learned to write, as everybody does nowadays ; and if his spelling was shaky, that was only what might be expected of his rank ; and after all, spelling is a very modern fad. Such spelling as he used was largely phonetic, reproducing that dialect of London English which his Lordship affected.

For these various causes it was that the paper at which he stared with an as yet inquisitive expression ran thus :

" If the Government get in furst, wot price yrs trooly ?

If this child gets in furst, wot'll they do ?

Fifty-fifty for Fatty.

Worsing."

It is a tribute to Lord Delisport's unique powers of analysis that in these brief sentences all the essential elements of a highly complicated situation were set down. He could see the problem, and he kept on staring at it. But that was not the same as solving it.

At last he did two things to stimulate his genius. He took a large gulp of neat whisky out of a flask which he habitually carried ; and he got up from his chair and began to pace up and down the room.

It was a very large room, and as Lord Delisport was one of those modern men of affairs who appreciate the value of beauty in their surroundings, he had had it completely furnished as a replica of the Oak Room at Andhamhurst Abbey. Messrs. Delavigne, to whom he had given the contract, had been so conscientious as to include copies of the Holbein and of the anonymous Jacobean portrait in the original. The effect was the more striking as the windows of the office looked out on a goods yard of a large railway; for Lord Delisport could not bear the noises of the street, and had determined to have his Holy of Holies at the back of the great building. As for the shunting of trucks, the hooting and whistling of engines, the grinding of wheels on rails, the enormous gasps of steam, and the rest of it, they soothed Lord Delisport. They reminded him of his earlier years, when he also had worked upon the line at that shamefully low wage. The contrast between then and now delighted him.

He stared at the goods yard for some seconds with his hands in his trousers pockets, then he began pacing up and down the room again and studying the problem in his own mind.

The whole Rotarian motion power in industry and transport was now more and more dependent on Durandite and therefore upon Eremin. The only really large deposit of Eremin known under paying conditions was in that tangled frontier line between the new Annihilationist Republic of West Irania, which Moscow had set up after the collapse of Turkish resistance, and the boundaries of Iraq. Apart from the Californian deposits, which were rapidly nearing exhaustion, there were two other small patches hitherto discovered both in very similar country, one on the barren slopes of the Andes, and another in the high mountains at the source of the Mekong. But the proposition of ore in the first was not at the paying level, and, in the second, transport was prohibitive. The Durandite figures in connection with marine transport have gone up, as everybody knows, in the most extraordinary fashion. It already looks as though the new invention might supplant every other form of power at sea. The figures of machines equipped for Durandite in the last five years have been under 4,000, 15,000, 18,270, and last year a sudden jump to 83,000, measured in Davidson's units.

Lord Delisport knew all that. His mighty intelligence had concluded that the material essential

for such an industry would be in increasing demand,
and the fact that this one and only means of this
stuff—apparently inexhaustible—was concentrated
in one place in the small republic of West Irania
suggested a monopoly. He proposed to secure
that monopoly for his own group and the German
groups with which it was interlocked.

The Republic of West Irania was Annihilationist.
Moscow was always denying responsibility when
responsibility was awkward, and always affirming
its protection when protection was needed. Anyhow,
he would take it that this concession once granted
would hold. When the Agent for the Republic of
West Irania gave the concession, if the claim to
territory held good, the Moscow Government would
see that the bargain was observed. They had
done so with Tomkinson in the Manchurian affair,
and they had done so with that French firm in
Turkestan—they were getting a reputation for such
reliability.

He stopped in his pacing up and down and
considered the snag in his way. If by any method
best known to themselves the politicians wangled
that bit of land into the mandated territory before
the concession was passed, he was done. He
feared one other rival, a Mr. Angus Worsing of

Glasgow and the Castle, Glenaber; a man of whom the public heard little, for he disliked publicity, but who was one of the most powerful forces in England, having behind him not only his own great organisation, but the Holman Bank and all it stood for in the United States.

The Worsing difficulty he would tackle later. For the moment the essential thing was to forestall his own Government with its greedy effort to secure that Eremin for itself, and, incidentally, for the British Navy as well as the carrying trade. They might have nobbled it already! It made his blood run cold. For a moment he thought of bringing in Italian Influence as a counterweight. Italy was the one great claimant who might if it chose call a halt. It dominated Asia Minor and its influence there marched with Irak and West Irania. Only, Italy must not get it. He would have to use influence personally and make it worth while for someone in power at Rome to raise the question just enough to provide delay and yet to bamboozle his Chief the Head of the State. Should he start for Rome that very day? . . . No . . . he thought better of it.

Lord Delisport lived in wholesome awe of the Italian Government. For nearly sixty years it had grown in strength and the Italian nation with it, now possessed of colonies " mandated " from older Powers. He did not understand how it worked. It puzzled him. But he knew that what he would have called " approaches " were singularly difficult in the new Italy ; and that its Government had a ferocious and rapid way of acting very disrespectfully to foreign capitalists. It had even been known to put rich men in prison ; a thing inconceivable in happier lands. He took another turn up and down the room . . . It narrowed itself down to this . . . He must get at the Agent here, himself, and with the least delay.

The Agent who was coming to negotiate had passed through America. He knew that. He had got it through the usual channel. He was on his way to, or had just reached, England. But under what name he would pass, at what exact date he would (or had) come, Lord Delisport was still ignorant. Yet it was essential to get hold of him before the official world did. He pondered upon how that advantage was to be obtained. So he took one more turn up the room, and, as is the habit of genius, one more gulp of whisky out of his flask and, so fortified, sat down at last to act. The gulp of whisky had suggested an Avenue of Approach.

He took up the telephone, and pulled out his watch at the same time. It was not yet eleven.

He rang up a little public house on the other side of the river, and when he had got it he had to wait longer than he liked ; but he did not tap with his foot, nor waggle the holder up and down, as you and I might have done. These great Masters of the Modern World are masters of themselves.

After a pause he heard the voice, and he was glad to find it was that of Tommy himself : Tommy, his old mate of years ago, when they had worked side by side in the railway yards. For it was a pleasing trait in Lord Delisport's character that he did not neglect all his old friends. Indeed, it was by Lord Delisport's help that poor Tommy had been able to buy the little business of the Coal Wharf Arms and serve drink to the sailors who frequented it. He had been provided with the capital after a little conversation some years back when he and Lord Delisport, then plain Mr. Goodge and only beginning to make good, had re-called anecdotes of old times, some of them not wholly to the wealthier man's advantage.

To-day it was the other way about. It was no longer Tommy who could squeeze him, it was rather Lord Delisport who had the power now to prevent the police acting against Tommy upon information received, and in natural gratitude Tommy would do odd jobs for his protector, or alternatively suffer the consequences—which he didn't want to.

Tommy's instructions over the telephone that morning were simple. He was to find out whether the Home Office was acting in a particular direction, and if so what that direction was and who the gentleman might be and where.

And who so willing as Tommy? Lord Delisport put up the receiver fairly sure of getting his information in time.

*   *   *   *

There sat in a Government Department a Minor Official. His was not the lordly part. He knew nothing of week-ends in the country houses of the great; he was not sent down with a large margin for expenses to meet important strangers at seaports; he was not even allowed to hold up the traffic in the Strand, nor to draw up minutes on fools in Hyde Park; his but to do and die. He would die in time, like the rest of us; and the doing consisted in writing out stuff all day long; and all day long; and all day long; and day by day. And for this he was paid an insufficient salary.

He was typing out on this particular day of God a copy of the report which Mr. Palmer had written out. He was taking down the report on Richard Mallard to put it on the files.

It is worth noting that whereas things of this kind when they are strictly secret and confidential are copied in duplicate by the insertion of a carbon between the top page and the second, a third copy is rarely made. But on this occasion the Minor Official was at the pains of inserting a second carbon, so that a third, rather blurred copy, should be created. It was the end of his day, and he was off to take a cup of tea with a friend at a neighbouring corner. He carefully filed the first copy and the second in their proper places; the third he put in his pocket.

He and the friend met and drank together their infusions of the oriental drug. They discussed affairs at large, the climate, the professional politicians, the murders, and the rest. But the hour for taking suburban trains was approaching, and the Minor Official and his friend lived in widely distant homes, he in Ealing, but the other on the south side of the river at the Coal Wharf Arms. It was necessary to get to the root of the matter quickly, and the friend said :

" Well, anythink more abaht it ? "

And the Minor Official said doubtfully : " Yes, not much."

" Then," said the friend, " yer 've not got a bit of paper pr'aps yer could show me ? "

" No," said the Minor Official. " I can only tell you what I've heard." He held that piece of paper in reserve. Pieces of paper are damning evidence.

" Well, what's that ? " said the friend. He was anxious to get back to the bar ; he didn't wholly trust his potman. He had a suspicious nature, had Tommy, the fruit of misfortune.

" Precious little." The Minor Official looked over his shoulder to make certain that they were not overheard. So did Tommy. In his trade one has to be careful. They waited until the waitress had moved off to another table. Then the Minor Official added rapidly in a very low voice :

" Name, Richard Mallard ; stopping Titanic. Going to Scotland. Back to Stratford—don't know which Stratford. Government on to him, of course. That's all."

" That's orl ? " said Tommy, with an appearance of disappointment. He had only got half of what he wanted for his master. " Yer can't say as they've nabbed 'im, 'ave they ? " and he jerked his

thumb towards Westminster, where the Great
confer upon the affairs of England.

The Minor Official shook his head. "They've
seen him. I've not heard what he's said."

"Well, fat lot of use you are," grumbled Tommy.
"Going to Scotland, is he?" He picked up both
bills. "D'yer know *when* he's going to Scotland by
any chance? D'yer know *that?*"

The Minor Official again looked round furtively,
and said rapidly, in a whisper: "No!" (which,
after all, was not very valuable information).

"Fat lot o' use," replied the disgruntled Tommy.
But he passed an envelope to the other under the
table, paid for both—fourpence in all—and, as Mr.
John Stuart Mill majestically remarks in his
Treatise on Bills of Exchange, "the transaction
was at an end."

How simple, after all, is the machinery of the
Great Democracy of which we have the privilege to
be citizens! Administrations may have been leaky
in an older and more wicked time, but to-day they
are watertight and incorruptible, because they are
by the People, of the People and for the People.

*   *   *   *

The resources of civilisation—that is, of Tommy—

were by no means exhausted. There was no more
to be had out of the Minor Official, but the Great,
unlike the rest of us, can get domestics. The Home
Secretary had faithful and devoted ones in
considerable numbers, and one was of Tommy's
acquaintance. He had seen to that shortly after
the formation of the present administration. He
reluctantly let the bar and the doubtful potman
slide for the moment (why couldn't old Goodge get
these things done in closing time ?) and sought
that friend. It was a nice move. Yes, old Mossy
Face (such was the playful term used for Sir Henry
Hardham by the faithful and devoted ones of his
domestic staff) *had* met this fellow Mallard, only
last night at Mother Corvan's. He'd heard old
Mossy Face talking it over at lunch, he had. He'd
gone to meet him at dinner that very evening at
his niece's. Did he know what happened ? Was
it likely ! Had old Mossy Face said nothing that
evening ? Only talking to himself like ; kept on
muttering about a young fool's obstinacy and
someone who was play-acting. It might be Mary
Gorman ; some of those Toffs were sweet on her,
and you never knew with old fools like Mossy Face.
And that was all the faithful and devoted one
knew.

He wondered why Tommy thanked him so warmly and why he was in such a hurry to be off.

In just under the minute Tommy was in the public telephone box and had rung up the Empire Builder. In a quarter of an hour, at the grudged expense of a taxi-cab (but he'd double it on the Exes) he was back at the Coal Wharf Arms.

*　　　　*　　　　*　　　　*

Lord Delisport, where the majesty of big business was concerned, was as tenacious as a lover or an athlete. He waited there patiently for the hour and the quarter, almost the hour and the half. It was not his habit to hang on so long in the morning, but he found plenty to do with his secretary and his papers. Just on half-past twelve came, after so many others, the one telephone call for which he had waited; the thick voice of Tommy; music in his ears!

It gave him the name—the name of Richard Mallard; the hotel—the Titanic; it told him of the plan for going to Scotland (when, he didn't know) and of Stratford afterwards; couldn't say which Stratford. The Home Secretary had seen him at Lady Corvan's only the night before. No, he didn't know if they'd clinched, but he thought *not* from the way the Home Secretary had muttered about obstinacy that morning. But he couldn't be sure. That was all.

Then was it seen with what rapidity the British Man of Big Business (interlocked with the German Group) can jerk. Lord Delisport, within a brief quarter of an hour, had rung off Tommy, rung up Another Number ; got the wrong number ; nearly had a fit ; got on to Another Number all right ; made an appointment with the Another Number to come to Delisport House in Hill Street that afternoon at 3.0, and given the Another Number his usual instructions to present himself as a messenger with a parcel ; rung off the Another Number ; called for the Titanic ; got a wrong number, nearly had a second fit ; got on to the Titanic at last ; thought better of it, and cut off and hung up the receiver without even giving his name ; looked feverishly at his watch ; was horrified to find it was nearly one ; shouted for his car at once ; squirmed in agony during three long blocks in the traffic, and was in the Titanic at exactly 1.23. He asked boldly for Mr. Mallard. He had no time to lose !

Mr. Mallard was in. What luck ! But then, he always had luck ! Richard Mallard was lunching gloomily by himself, wondering horribly what the day would bring forth, and lo ! the day had brought forth the card of Lord Delisport, which was brought to him at his table. He looked at it at first in doubt. Then the full meaning of that famous name burst upon him. He jumped up. He must go out and see him at once. He was deeply impressed.

Richard Mallard had no acquaintance with the Peerage of the United Kingdom of Great Britain and Ireland, save through the Cinema in Havana.

That admirable instrument of general education had left him with a very vivid impression, as we saw in an earlier chapter, of the Palaces these Beings inhabit.

It had left him with an even more vivid impression of the features with which a respectful Creator has blessed them : the long, dignified face ; the scanty, well-groomed grey hair ; the deep, tragic, but proudly restrained eyes ; and above all, that dominant aquiline nose so clearly predestined for the summits of the social world.

Judge, then, of his surprise when he discovered, as might a man over whom you have thrown a bucket of cold water, the Lord Delisport of reality contrasted with the Lord Delisport of his very brief dream.

Now you, O most intelligent reader, pride your-self (if you pride yourself on anything) upon your mastery of psychology. And you are right. But you would be an even worse psychologist than I am if you could not guess what went on in the young man's mind when the Marquis approached him with that remarkable smile of greeting which had been of such profound effect upon statesmen of every party, and even his colleagues in the financial worlds of London and Berlin. It was not something wrong about Delisport, that he did not look the part; *that* did not trouble the Ingenuous Boy; rather did he rapidly invest the concrete Baron at once with the abstract qualities of his order, and though the thin, firm lips were thick and blobby, the tragic eyes twinkling with cunning, and the aquiline nose more like a small champagne cork, none the less there shone through these mere mortal things the inner divinity of the House of Lords—so true is it that the spirit, not the body, makes the man.

The sublime figure advanced towards him with arms outstretched ; the mouth spoke.

" Mistur Mallud, I persume ? "

" Yes, that's my name, eh ? " said the other, hoping he was using the right English and doing the right things.

"Ye'll ex-coose me droppin' in like without an invite?"

"Oh, I'm sure," murmured the Victim, very truthfully, "it's an honour! What?" And he timidly took the outstretched hand.

"It's not 'igh breedin'," said his lordship "takin' yer sudden like this, but I'm *keen*, yer know! T's like this. Let's sit down and be comfy. 'Ad lunch?"

"Yes, sir—my lord, Lord Delisport, I mean."

They sank into two deep chairs.

"Ah! Then it'll be coffee. And something *with* it," and the Empire Maker dug the Cuban in the right rib and winked violently. The jab was a smart one, but coming from such a source it was well worth it, resembling the lover's pinch of which William Shakespeare has well remarked that it hurts but is desired.

"Chartroose," he continued, to the waiter. "Yeller?" he said, turning to his companion.

"Oh, yes, anything, what?" said Richard, a little too rapidly, in his confusion.

"Wot's say?"

"I said 'yellow,'" repeated the other, blushing.

"Yeller, then two of 'em, with two cups o' coffee, and look sharp will yer?"

It arrived. The nobleman proceeded.

" As I was a-saying, it's like this. I want to talk
business. Naow, you'll think me 'urried, like, but
I'm a business man, I am. The moment I 'eard as
you'd landed, I says to myself, ' me for 'im,' that's
what I says. And now yer know why I'm 'ere."
And he winked again portentously. " Naow, first
of all, Mistur Mallud, we want to get straight on
this. I'm losing no time, yer see, can't help that !
Best for both on us ! Ter begin with, anyhow !
De-tails, why ! we can see to 'em later." He
lowered his voice, " We must come to business, eh ?
Yer know *my* business and I know *yours,* eh ? "
He leant forward, bending a very direct look upon
the dazed face before him, and beginning the serpent
and bird act. " Is there anythink doin' ? That's
what *I* want ter know."

The inhabiting fear popped its ugly little head out
in Richard Mallard's heart. Could it be that this
unknown though great man was yet Another of
Them ? The next words confirmed his anxiety.

" Because, if there *is* anythink doin', why I'm
the man to do it with yer," and the speaker slapped
his thigh with decision. He had always heard that
great fortunes depended upon rapid dealing ; his
own great fortune hitherto had proved it. And
he was not departing from the lesson he had learnt.

" Naow, see 'ere," he went on, seeing Mallard's mouth opening undecidedly, and determined to bear down any opposition, " yer may think I'm what they call 'brupt and *cassong*, as I've 'eard it called—but then, that's yours truly. And it's the best way, ain't it, arter all ? You knows 'oo *I* am," he said again with innocent pride, " and I knows 'oo *you* are. So that's that. Now, then, Mistur Mallud, anythin' doin' ? "

"If you mean, you know—I mean," began the other.

" Yus," broke in the Master Builder with decision. " That's wot I *do* mean. All I say is—wot price ? " he put up a hand. " Naow, I don't want to rush yer, I'm not so foolish as to think you'll give me a figure hen and two sticks like. All I want to know is, is anything doin ? "

" You see . . ." began Mallard again, " I have already told the . . ." Then the fear of Public Powers took possession of him, and he rapidly changed his phrase. " Other people already . . . But I didn't see how . . . . ."

" Other people ? " snapped Delisport suspiciously. " Yer don't mean . . ." and he jerked his head sideways, and his thumb over his shoulder. " Not our friend the canny Scot ? Not Scotland, anyway ? "

"I don't see what Scotland can have to do with it," said the other in amaze.

"Ar, you're a deep un!" answered the admiring Peer. "Naow you give me your word yer weren't thinking of Scotland?"

"Eh, Scotland? I mean to say . . . No, Scotland's got nothing to do with it, what?"

"I take it the canny Scot's out of it?" (Lord Delisport could not conceal his relief.)

"But if you mean the rights in the place—well, to be plain, if you mean . . ."

"'Ush!" said Lord Delisport, in a voice dramatically lower, and looking round him. "I'm all for business in a public place—'leviates suspicion, I say; but, oh Lord! Mistur Mallud, no nimes! No nimes, I do beg and pray, no nimes!"

"Well, sir," continued Mallard, "the point is that I have already been approached."

Delisport nodded. "The Gov'ment," he whispered thickly.

"Why, yes—to be quite plain—you know—I think it was for the Government. But I had to tell them the only thing I can say to you too, which is, don't you know, that really I don't see how, until I've consulted with them over there at home and got more details, about . . ."

" 'Ush, 'ush ! " urged his lordship again. He rose suddenly and added, " Yer've got a room 'ere ? Sitting-room ? Let's go there. It'll be more private like."

" By all means, what ? " said the young man, and with a heavy heart he led the way, while Lord Delisport lit one of those large cigars which helped him to arrange his thoughts.

For full fifteen minutes did the Empire Builder in that sitting-room attempt to get some definite word. No definite word could the sufferer pronounce save the same old litany, that he had no right yet— that it didn't seem honest—and even the absurd remark, reiterated, that anyhow he didn't think it was worth anything, what ? He hadn't heard anything to make him think so, you know. And he had to wait anyhow, till they could send him information—eh ? Otherwise he wouldn't know what he was doing, would he—what ?

And all the while he was in such an increasing fever of worry and anxiety that he could hardly frame his words. He stood up, fingering the mantel-shelf nervously, over-topping his temporary guest by a head, yet dominated by him. There raced through his mind the thought that he was now in peril of making two enemies, one this powerful

Master of Millions, with whose name the Press had made him familiar even beyond the seas, and the other what he conceived to be the yet more powerful body of men known as His Britannic Majesty's Government.

Oh, dear ! What had he done to deserve all this ? He wished to God for the hundredth time in his life, but from a new angle, that the "Mallard Millions" had never been heard of. And this was the quiet England he had so longed for !

As he stood there sweating in the agony of the thought, and still tapping absurdly at the mantelpiece with his distracted fingers, Lord Delisport took his rising as a signal of dismissal. No, dismissal from another man's room was something which the great man never accepted. He was in manners as in everything a High Man of Our Time. He made it a rule whenever anyone, great or small, hinted that an interview was at an end to prolong it by a few moments, that he might show who was master ; and so he did on this occasion.

He stood there with his cigar cocked up at an angle, fixing his eyes upward upon that innocuous and troubled young face, and he muttered twice, " Oh, yer're a downy one, *you* are ! But I can see through yer ! "

Lord Delisport musing upon the profundity of Mr. Mallard

Then, when he thought he had lingered long enough to impress a man probably not very wealthy —as yet—but one whom he must not—as yet— offend too much, he moved to the door, and as he did so held out the hand of friendship.

" Well, Mistur Mallud," he ended, " I must be orf ! We don't seem to have got much farther, but we've broken the ice, eh ? Now, I'll see yer again, shan't I ? Eh ? We can talk abaht it then. And mean- while I 'm clear o' one thing. None of this Scotch business, eh ? See you later." And while Mallard answered something incoherent, he was gone.

But as he passed the Enquiry Clerk downstairs on his way out Lord Delisport asked a certain question, waited a moment, was handed a slip of paper with pencil jottings on it, put ten shillings unobtrusively into the giver's hand, and passed through the revolving doors of the Titanic to his car.

*   *   *   *

It was striking three. The trouble in Richard Mallard's soul had increased to a fever. Lord Delisport was back at Delisport House interviewing Another Number who had come there to his appoint- ment, with a parcel in his hand and whistling to the Area Gate and had been shown up from the Basement.

And who was Another Number whom so powerful a man was thus intent on seeing ? It was a certain acquaintance of his upon whom he placed a firm because well-tried reliance.

A bony figure, hardly taller than his own, with a strong, somewhat sullen mouth, a nose that turned up somewhat, and eyes which were kept most of the time half-closed, faced the Marquis. It showed some respect for its master, but not much, standing with its hands in its jacket pockets in an habitual gesture. It was taking orders.

I could quote fifty things to show the depth and power of Lord Delisport's intelligence ; but as the modern world is crawling and hissing with men of this kind, and as you will be familiar with their abilities, I will quote only this : A lesser man would have recourse, where private enquiry was concerned, to some office which regularly undertakes that very necessary and highly-developed activity of modern life. Lord Delisport was too wise. He had his own staff of Sleuths, and that evening he was dealing with the Sleuth whom he trusted most.

I should be betraying his lordship's most intimate secrets and doing him a very bad turn if I gave you

his real name. I will not do so. For the matter of
that, I do not know it. But I have seen the
gentleman a dozen times in Public Houses, in the
Lobby outside the House of Lords, in Ballrooms
pursuing in various costumes his interesting trade.
We will call him Sleuth A.

He had been picked out quite young by Sir George
Goodge, Bart., for all the qualities which make
the perfect Follow-Up. But most of all for the
ability with which he could conceal the social
origins from which he sprang.

For Sleuth A was the son of a clergyman in the
Midlands, long dead, who had starved himself to
give the boy a good education ; and when the
young fellow had been thus picked out for higher
work he was already articled to a good firm of
solicitors in the City.

But to see Sleuth A lounging, in carefully-selected
costume, at the bar of a lesser public house in
Mayfair, picking up information on the rich from
their menials, you would never have dreamt of
his nurture. It was a miracle of transformation !
Now a man, argued his employer, who can so dress
and act, in one capacity, can dress and act in any
other. Nor had he been disappointed. Sleuth A
was well worth his £12 a week—and pickings. He

was even on the way to blackmail and still higher things.

*　　　　*　　　　*　　　　*

Lord Delisport crouched on his low, padded chair beneath the two great Chinese Vases (which were of the Ming Dynasty) peered with small, close, comprehending eyes upon the notes before him.

"He's going to the Lakes . . . so far as I can see," and here he turned over a page, "yes, 'ere it is. The man at the 'otel reports that 'e takes the 10.50 from Euston . . . Yer've got to tike yer ticket and yer place. Be on the platform 'alf-past." He looked up sharply. "Yer know his fice?"

"Yes, Me'Lord," replied Sleuth A, as deferential as he could bring himself to be.

"Right-o, boy! Now yer watch for 'im. 'E'll be going somewhere in what they call The Lakes— yer'll pay on from Lancaster. Jes' foller."

"Yes, Me'Lord."

"Whenever 'e stops, yer let me know. Ef 'e goes on north, yer'll let me know. And yer'll *foller*. And min' that! Yer *foller*."

"Yes, Me'Lord."

Sleuth A : being the Private Detective specially chosen
by Lord Delisport for his power to hide his
true social origins

"None of yer writing! Ring up."

"Yes, Me'Lord."

"What'll yer warnt?"

"It'll cost twenty pound, Me'Lord, at least," said Sleuth A with determination. "Of course, as usual, I 'll give you an account."

"Oh, damn t' 'count!" said the millionaire. "Twenty's cheap, Gawd knows, if yer pull it off . . And if yer *don't* . . ." Here he leered, and the man at whom he leered replied with a slight nod. "Whoy . . ." continued the Peer, and he leered up again humorously, and he made a move with his boot, signifying the Sack, but betraying (though he did not know he did so) some little fear of what gentlemen call Pressure, but affected people The Turn of the Screw. For, indeed, Sleuth A knew by this time a good deal about Lord Delisport.

"Very good, Me'Lord," answered Sleuth A with an imperceptible bow. And that was that.

CHAPTER VII

On his uneasy bed Richard Mallard had known what young men should never know. It was not a mere uneasy night such as he had already passed immediately before. It was sheer insomnia. He tossed in a mental agony and stared at the black darkness.

Was this what he had promised himself ? Was this the quiet England of tradition and culture and all the rest of it ? The culture of the films ? . . . He was hunted . . . He was a hare, and the hounds were invisible . . . Go where he would, it was the same abominable business, worse with every passing hour ; unknown grandees asking him to dine in order to torture him ; unknown shadowers following him at every turn ; unknown millionaires turning up and growing more insolent with the moments that passed, and that though they were Peers—a combination to which his brain could not adjust itself. Cabinet Ministers and Secretaries of Cabinet Ministers, police cells, fiendish magistrates who somehow became suddenly friendly . . . more shadowing—a suspicion of every soul that breathed.

He could not sleep. He sat up and stared into the night. By all of which you may see that Richard Mallard was not only of a futile but of a highly nervous temperament ; and for all I know it was the result of transferring a human organism (blessed word !) from the Gulf of Mexico to this our Island Home.

An hour of this was bad enough ; but after an hour he began to grow sane. After all, what could they do to him ? He was right to wait for details ; he was right to refuse any bargain until he knew what they had to say. But whether he were right or wrong, damn it, you know, he was a free man, and Magna Charta, and all that—what ?

And anyhow, next day he would repose. Next day it would be all over, for it was his date for leaving London. He had got his place booked and his ticket. At last he would be alone !

He had landed here to see sights like a lamb ; he had planned to go to the Lakes before the Highlands and then to Stratford-on-Avon as they all do. He had read his Wordsworth dutifully aboard the steamer ; he had his maps ; he even had the name of his little hostelry, the "Black Horse," all noted down. It was where Wordsworth (so the guide-book told him) had written that immortal poem which opens like a trumpet-call :

> "I will not go to Windermere to-day,
> To-morrow will be more convenient."

Richard Mallard, on the other hand, *would* go to Windermere—or at any rate to the "Black Horse." I have said on a previous page that he was fed up to the molars upon that previous occasion ; but now since the Delisport affair he was fed up to the tonsils. Yea, to the very gullet. And now it was over ! The very next day he would be off and his freedom would begin.

Relieved by that conclusion, he fell into a better sleep. Poor innocent !

*   *   *   *

Forty minutes before Richard Mallard left in his taxi for Euston Sleuth A had gone off in Lord Delisport's much more comfortable car for the same terminus. They travelled up together, some carriages apart ; and at Lancaster Sleuth A had discovered how far he was to pay on.

They got out together at the wayside station ;

13

but Sleuth A had no luggage save a very small
and dirty handbag, and he did not make himself
conspicuous. There was a fly waiting from the
" Black Horse." Richard Mallard climbed into it.
Sleuth A followed quite a quarter of an hour
afterwards, on foot.

*　　　　*　　　　*　　　　*

The " Black Horse " on the shores of Windermere is
one of the four hundred and seventy-three unknown
little wayside inns of England which are in every
guide-book. They even kept up the phrase " Ye
Blacke Horse " until 1935, when for very shame
they had to spell it properly. It had been visited
by the last French Prime Minister when he fled to
England before being guillotined forty years ago,
and happier men and women from the United
States had gloried to sleep in the bed which Queen
Elizabeth herself (as they were told) had graced—
but it was a lie. At any rate, Richard Mallard
was at peace, and for the first time in all these days.
He had shaken everything off. He was rid of
them.

He found the " Black Horse " a very heaven.
After all, he was from beyond the Atlantic, and

evil would be the heart that grudged him the sham
black oak, the grandfather's clock, the warming-pan,
Old Uncle Tom Cobley and All.

Moreover this place was owned by the Amalgamated
Imperial Brewery Company of which most of the
shares are owned by the British Investment Trust
Limited, of which a controlling interest lies in
Pagman's Cheese, Dairy and General, of which the
bulk is held by the Caledonian Securities Averaging
Association, of which most of the Deferred Preference,
all the Debentures and 51% of the ordinary are in
the possession of Angus Worsing, Esquire, of Glasgow
and the Castle, Glenaber.

With what pleasure had not that ubiquitous
gentleman learned (through his card indices) that
a Richard Mallard had selected this, out of so many
similarly controlled hotels for his sojourn in England's
Noblest Shrine of Natural Beauties ; and how well
be could trust in his Manager and Manageress to
report. What wonder either that under such
supervision Richard Mallard could feel that he had
arrived in the true, the profound, the reposeful, the
Ancient England !

Yes ! This at last was England ! He made warm
friends with the landlady, the landlord—Manager,
I mean—their children, the man who waited on

him at table (and what a table !—I mean, what cooking ! I mean, what horrible cooking !) the maids (from London), the ostler (on ticket-of-leave), and the man who leant against the post outside and also was so unimportant that he only served the local police for a bob a shot.

Richard Mallard told them all, and particularly the landlady, that he meant to go on to Scotland. He even gave them the date ; the hotel in the Highlands beyond Glasgow to which his guide-book recommended him ; the " Clan Tarroch." He was the companion of all the world.

In and out of the bar of the " Black Horse " lounged that deplorable lounger day after day. He was looking for work and he didn't find it. He seemed to have enough money for beer. And to men he was known by no name ; but to the gods he was Sleuth A.

Oh ! How Richard Mallard delighted in that little inn. At last he drew the breath of freedom ! It was a relief from pressure like that of a man disemprisoned. No one turned up unexpectedly with sudden demands. No one desired his favour. He did not find the same unknown face two or three times running at the corner of the street, and —too good to be true—he was free of all big houses.

He was of the Middle Class again, and he thanked God for it.

Into such a period of relaxation there came one slightly jarring exception ; but only one. He had written down his name in that large, frank, colonial writing of his, as our modern machinery of highly organised police system demands, upon the register of the hotel. And it gave him no pleasure to observe on the very first night a bar lounger talking with a broad local accent and turning for amusement to the hotel register just at closing time after he had finished his drinks, running a dirty finger down the list of names, and stopping suddenly at his own as though to certify it. It seemed incongruous. But when the fellow shut the book again and said good night in tones which burst with local honesty he was half reassured. Yet, after all, what the devil was this passion for looking at names ? Perhaps it was a habit of the Lakes. They have little to do up there. As for Sleuth A, he had a reason for what he had done. And what reason was that, you ask, bewildered reader ? Oh ! reader of small experience, it was to know under what name the agent for West Irania chose to pass. He was glad to find it was still Mallard. It made things easier.

From the little Post Office two miles away Sleuth A telephoned to Delisport House. Mallard he said, was the name still kept, and Scotland indeed the next step. He had seen no trace of anyone here to meet him. He was going to the Clan Tarroch Hotel. Thence he would telephone again.

On the night before Richard Mallard started for Scotland he packed his bag in a complete peace of mind. The past was forgotten. The absurd nightmare of mystery had sunk away.

These few days in the peace (or whatever it is) that haunts the lonely hills (if that is the right phrase), those trailing clouds of glory (I'm sure of that), the something or other that is in setting suns, the depth and not the tumult of the soul (Wordsworth), the warming-pan, the grandfather's clock, the four-posters, the outrageous bills, the blasted cooking, the ceaseless rain, the crowds of trippers—all these had formed his lullaby, and he was once again the care-free, not very rich, travelling, touring, independent Richard Mallard. He went to bed early to dream of beauty born of murmuring sound (or whatever it is) and of the Bonny Bonny Banks and Annie Laurie that lay a-head.

On that same night, after Richard Mallard had gone to his early couch of Chippendale, there sauntered into the "Black Horse" a gentleman of a perfect exterior — sleek, smooth, demure. He kept a hired motor waiting at the door. He took no room at the "Black Horse;" he did not even take supper—though he had taken four free drinks. But what he did of most consequence was to enter into some considerable conversation with the land-lady, and even with the landlord. They understood each other perfectly. There was no occasion for the sleek, the smooth, the demure to apologise for not taking a room at the "Black Horse." All was quite understood. He went back (after learning what he had to learn) to his motor, and drove off to sleep that night at a station a little way up the line where the train stopped to pick up passengers and was hitched at Carlisle on to the express for Glasgow.

Late the same evening the Bar Lounger padded out from his humble lodging to yet another station a little way up the line, where the train also stopped to pick up passengers and was hitched at Carlisle on to the express for Glasgow. In the public house opposite that station he stopped. Both he and the Sleek One had it in mind to take the train for Scotland next morning: for Glasgow; nay, more, to arrive at or near this Clan Tarroch Hotel in the Highlands.

Such is the complexity of human affairs that neither of these two knew of the existence of the other. Yet must I confess to my intelligent reader that not only was the Bar Lounger most undoubtedly Sleuth A, but the well-to-do and educated person, sleek, smooth, demure, was Sleuth B.

And pray of whom was Sleuth B the Sleuth?

Why, to tell you the honest truth, he was the Sleuth of that remarkable share-shuffler, I mean Commercial Magnate, Angus Worsing, Esq. . . . . not even knight. But Angus Worsing could buy up your Knights. And Angus Worsing was on to Eremin. And Angus Worsing was on to Mallard— oh! He'd been on to Mallard for days.

It had taken him a little time, but he had got on to him. He had got on to him good and hard. He had worked along a different line from his great rival the Delisport; but by this time he knew at least as much as that great rival; and hence the presence in the Scotch Express of Sleuth B quietly smoking in a first class carriage, while Sleuth A in a third class carriage, also smoking (but a clay pipe), used the occasion to play Nap with sundry passengers and to make three and sixpence in the first hour.

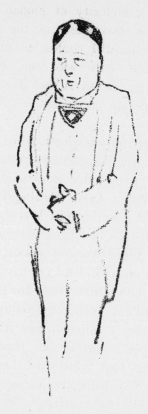

Sleuth B: being the Private Detective specially chosen by Mr. Worsing for his power to conceal his true social origins

The train pulled up at Dale Water, the station for the "Black Horse." From a first class carriage Sleuth B looked out discreetly, and made sure that Richard Mallard had entered the train. Sleuth A, from far away back towards the tail of it, looked out boldly with a hard face and made equally sure, both of them. And the train rolled on.

So Richard Mallard was bound for the Clan Tarroch Hotel, the Pearl of the Highlands, beyond Glasgow, and so was Sleuth A, and so was Sleuth B. And Sleuth B having taken the elementary step of informing Mr. Worsing by telephone of the name of that magnificent hotel, Angus Worsing had very methodically decided to leave his flat— his princely flat—in the second metropolis of Scotland, and had secured a suite in the Clan Tarroch Hotel in the neighbouring Highlands, to be ready for so distinguished an arrival.

And at Carlisle the local train bearing Sleuth A, Sleuth B, and their distinguished *protégé* Richard Mallard was switched on to the express for Glasgow at 6.15, due to arrive at Glasgow Central Station at 8.20.

At dinner in the train, within two hours of Glasgow, Richard Mallard fell into conversation with a man of the sort with whom he felt instinctively at ease ;

a quiet, well-spoken, intelligent fellow, sleek, smooth, demure, with something about him of the marks of wealth, and with an interest in the West Indies which (once more) gave Richard Mallard a feeling of home.

It was to the experienced an interesting because impenetrable face upon which the young man gazed. For one thing, it was almost impossible to tell its age. It might be thirty — it might be fifty, or even more. It was of an even pale complexion, waxy or ivoried. The eyes were discreet, but intaking (I did not say " taking in "). The voice had a sub-Calvinistic accent. The hair was dark and very neatly parted and treated with some patent oleaginous mixture, at once a flattener and a tonic (like gin). His chin and neck were a little too ample. His hands were always at rest and often folded.

Had Richard Mallard known the world better he would at once have said to himself that Such a Being was designed by God for a minor position in the House of Commons. Happily for him, Richard Mallard did not know the world, and took his new acquaintance for what he said he was—a Man of Affairs. In point of fact he had been born the son of a coal-heaver, had adopted stage carpentering for his profession, had been remarked by Angus Worsing ten years before for his skill in impersonation when he had suddenly to take on the mute part of the Devil appearing in " The Haunted House " at a minor provincial theatre of Galloway, and had been lifted to his present exaltation and good salary by the same Angus Worsing's unerring eye for a fellow that could deceive.

The stranger was very frank in spite of his well-bred reserve ; he was (he said) a modest Liverpool merchant travelling to Glasgow on business.. His grandfather had had a great deal to do in the old days with the West Indian sugar trade, and the firm had been nearly ruined by modern changes, the use of Beet Sugar, the subsidies and all that. Now the business had been switched over to something quite different. It had gone African. But, reading the old letters, he had now and then thought that if he could ever get the leisure he would like to take one of those cruises of which he had read, upon a big liner, to that paradise of the West, the Antilles, and (on the way) to Cuba. With the word Cuba they became real friends and Richard Mallard spoke at large.

From big liners that took people on holidays they fell to talking over the coffee, as the train rattled on, of the ease of modern communications. From that to the curious exceptions in the same. Thereupon Richard Mallard could not but remark on the grievance he had in having to sleep that night in the great town of Glasgow, instead of going on to the Highland Hotel only fifty miles away in the hills. Surely the Company could have arranged a connection? he said. Especially for such a House as the Clan Tarroch—the Pearl of the Highlands.

His companion agreed, offering him a cigar, which was really very good, and refusing a liqueur offered him in return, "Because," said he, "I make it a rule." This remark (Richard himself could not have told you why) vaguely stirred in him some memory of the Home Secretary, but he put the unworthy thought aside, and said :—

"Well, it can't be helped. I should have liked to get in to the Clan Tarroch to-night, but if I can't I can't."

"The Clan Tarroch?" said his companion, with sudden animation. "Oh, but that's really interesting! That's where *I'm* making for! Won't you come in my car? It would save you a lot of trouble!"

Richard Mallard was overwhelmed with gratitude.

Sure enough, there met the train at the Central Station in Glasgow one of those very noble cars to which he was becoming lately too much accustomed. For a moment a shadow of worry passed over his mind again. He remembered Delisport. The motor recalled Big Business. He dismissed the superstitious worry, and with further thanks accepted this chance friend's lift.

*   *   *   *

I am afraid, my dear little readers, that most of you have never been a Sleuth. Indeed, the chances are that in your happy and sheltered existence most of you have hardly heard of such beings as Sleuths, though those of us who take the rough and tumble of this world know only too well that we are barging our way hourly through a very fog of Sleuths.

Anyhow, if you have been a Sleuth, you will sympathise deeply with Sleuth A, left stranded at the Central Station in Glasgow, and seeing his quarry roll off with *another* Sleuth, a sleek, smooth, demure acquaintance in a magnificent motor car. But Sleuth A knew whom he was serving ; he had plenty of money, and what is worth more than money—or at any rate leads to more money, in his profession—a staff college mind. He jumped into a taxi, and said briefly, "Half a crown a mile, and follow them *fast*."

Through the crowded streets of Glasgow, even at that hour in the evening, the chase could be kept in hand ; but when they got farther out on the highland road the cylinders began to tell.

However, there is a God in these affairs. And with the noise of an over-charged gun the great car, now almost out of sight, burst a tyre.

Sleuth A tapped sharply on the glass. His taxi stopped hard. " Crawl up to them," he said in a low voice to the driver. " Stop about a hundred yards behind, and put out your lights."

" I darre not put oot me lights," returned the law-abiding Caledonian.

Sleuth A put a one-pound note out through the window, and the Caledonian dared.

Out crept Sleuth A, and came sauntering up to the disabled car. The two gentlemen were pacing up and down, smoking cigarettes under the summer night, while Mr. Worsing's expensive chauffeur, in some disgust at such a task, was putting on the spare wheel.

" No help wanted," said the chauffeur brusquely to the proletarian Sleuth A.

" Ay, but I'll be asking ye naething," answered Sleuth A, in the musical accents of the Queen of the Clyde.

" And you'll be getting nothing," answered the lordly one, as he sweated at the jack. Then also did that lordly one, inspired by the aforesaid God, make the mistake that people always make. He said a word too much. He said, " We'll be in Clan Tarroch before you've tramped two miles on your uppers."

Heaven avenges itself on the insolence of the rich and befriends the poor ! Not that Sleuth A was poor, but he looked poor, which is all that's needed. And, as it was already dark, Heaven was deceived. It had befriended Sleuth A—under an error of pauperistic exterior. He had learnt all he wanted to learn. Sleuth B and his quarry would be in the Clan Tarroch Hotel that night. He went back to his darkened taxi and waited till the too rich car ahead had begun to purr again. He waited till its lights had turned the corner and were out of sight. Then did he bid his driver light up again, and before getting in he asked : " What is there at Clan Tarroch ! "

" There's just the hotel."

" Nothing else ? "

" There's my wife's mither, if ye want to know."

" Will she let a lodging ? "

" She will."

" Why, then, if you will drive me to your wife's mother you shall have the double fare at the price we arranged."

" 'Tis but a cottage," said the honest driver. And then, under the lights of his car, hesitated at the poverty of his fare. But Sleuth A gave him the money there and then.

" If you will drive me to your wife's mother," he said, in a new and suddenly educated voice, " and persuade her to take me in, as a lodger for a day or two, she can make her own price. And he added another pound to make certain. The Caledonian wondered whether he were driving a Prince in disguise ; but he asked no questions.

*　　　*　　　*　　　*　　　•

The grand car got to the Clan Tarroch Hotel, the Pearl of the Highlands (though but on the edge of them) in time for supper ; the clientele of the Pearl took five meals a day, and this was the last. But voluntary.

As Richard Mallard went through the hall, helped

14

out of the car by gorgeous servitors, surrounded by the heads of stags in plaster, by panoplies of arms from the Ruhr and by suits of mail from Birmingham, he felt half afraid of so much feudal splendour, and the distant wail of bag-pipes added to his awe.

There were portraits, too, let into the shiny panelling. One of Prince Charlie, which he hoped to be contemporary, and one of a Clan Tarroch of the Bruce's time, very fierce. And one of his reigning Majesty. The roof was of oak beams from the Baltic set on edge, high and blackened as with smoke ; carefully blackened by James Arthur and Co. of Golden Square, London ; and there were, amid the Claymores, Eight Targes—that is, shields.

This was better even than the "Black Horse!" How far away, how drowned, non-existent, were the miseries of his London nightmare ! This was still more England—I mean, Scotland.

Richard scrupulously dressed. He felt he was in a company and under a roof both of which demanded it, and he sought his new friend the sleek, the demure with a pathetic confidence. He found him in the lounge, talking to an elderly, spare, reserved man ; concentrated, a little hard, but with a thin and searching smile. They got up, both of them, at his approach.

" Mr. Mallard, may I introduce you to my friend,
Mr. Worsing ? " And Richard Mallard was introduced
to the stranger's friend, Mr. Worsing. It was the
most natural thing in the world.

" Worsing," explained pleasantly the sleek, the
demure, " is here for a holiday. I don't know
whether you are stopping long, but if you are, you
could not have anyone to give you a better idea of
the country."

Richard Mallard was stopping for a few days.
He was glad that he would have companionship,
and he looked on Mr. Worsing with a pleased and
simple eye. All that he saw was an elderly man
(old enough to be his father) with a rather too
earnest expression and a bony face which looked
into his own with anxious scrutiny ; for the rest,
good clothes, quiet, and all carefully groomed.

Now if Richard Mallard had known Europe, and
especially this island, better, or perhaps if he had
been older, but certainly if he had suffered, he would
have seen far more. He would have seen in Mr.
Worsing the virtues and the vices of his kind.
He would have seen a preoccupation with money,
not from greed but because the pursuit of riches
was the only serious activity he knew. Mr.
Worsing showed in every line of his taut body that,

whatever he had had to do, it would have absorbed him. He worked for work's sake—and it had never come to him as a real experience that there was any other work but accumulating a fortune. He knew indeed, after a pale, fantastic fashion, that there were men who wrote and even some who prayed, men who built and men who painted ; but he thought of them all as either too lazy or too ignorant of affairs or too light-headed to attend·to the principal affair of human life.   Yet here he made exceptions, for if a painter or writer or architect had made a moderate fortune he took it as a proof of excellence—he felt real respect.

Moreover, if he had known our world, Richard Mallard would have wondered how two men so different as Worsing and Delisport could both be in the same trade of share-shuffling.

The over-anxious and much-too-careful face, which was trying to understand his own and was caught wondering, was not unscrupulous. It was not base. Its owner played the modern game of over-reaching, betrayal and cozening, but played it strictly to the rule, and worked by a code which aped the old idea of honour. Angus Worsing could not have endured life if he had lost what he would have called his self-respect. It would have killed him. And the worst blow to self-respect such a man can suffer is loss of money, or failing to deceive, or allowing himself to be deceived. But the base weapons of that were to be used in business, and only in business, and only on the public or competitors, not on innocents unworthy of his sword-play.

Richard Mallard was safe with Angus Worsing. There would be no swindling, there would not even be threats.

Angus Worsing, as he stood there stiffly leaning and his eyes still boring deep into the problem before him, was puzzled to the degree of discomfort and almost of pain. He couldn't make out the young man in front of him. It was not at all what he had expected. He really knew mankind—which is more than Delisports or Politicians or even Bureaucrats do— and this Richard Mallard did not fit in with the Richard Mallard of his reports.

It was not the youth nor the simple looks of the Envoy from West Irania—it was something below it all : character.

Locked away in his despatch case upstairs Angus Worsing had all the Dossier of the affair—much more voluminous than Delisport's and the Home Office's and the Foreign Secretary's put together. He knew

the route travelled exactly, through Asia to Japan,
and Vancouver ; he even knew the place in the woods
where the Envoy had crossed the United States
boundary. He knew of the negotiations with the
Government, and, two days later, while Mallard was
still in the Lakes, he had received a brief note on
Delisport's failure—copied from the pocket diary of
that worthy.

He had had from Sleuth B a very close description
by letter of the air, the gait, the accent, the manner
of the disguise. He was prepared for good acting.
Nevertheless, the reality shocked him. It was too
real. Hardly, until he heard it from the young
man's own lips, would he be sure that there was
indeed the Asiatic, the man at whose disposal lay
the concession of those millions. . . .

That same evening at supper they made friends
and planned an excursion for the morrow. Worsing
invited Sleuth B, but Sleuth B, alas ! couldn't
come ; he had to be back in Glasgow next noon.
Nor was Worsing surprised, since he himself had
given the order. There would be time enough to
send for his employé when occasion might arise.
For some days he would enjoy Mallard's company
here. Most unlike the politicians and still more
unlike Lord Delisport, Angus Worsing was never in

Mr. Angus Worsing reading the riddle of
Mr. Richard Mallard

a hurry. In *Who's Who* you might read his recreation
—Fishing. He knew how to play the fish and when
to gaff and land. He took his time, and if ever he
admitted a sharp gesture, it was just at the precise
moment when it would tell : never too early.

For one day after another these two together
explored the hills and talked of all things. Mallard
naturally and volubly of Cuba, of his distresses in
the States, of the beauties of Britain. Worsing of
politics, of local history, even of religion. But not a
word did he say of Asia nor hint that he knew the
true name and origin—surely he was right ?—of the
tall, amiable and seeming futile young companion.

Once indeed towards the end of the week he turned
the conversation with strangely emphatic interest on
to Eremin and all its possibilities. He grew eloquent,
and shot a glance unobserved at Mallard. The gentle
brown eyes gave no response. Science, it seemed,
didn't interest the young fellow, and by the polite
replies he made he betrayed an ignorance of Eremin
which would have deceived an archangel.

Worsing came back from that walk musing. He
telephoned to Sleuth B in Glasgow and cross-
examined him at length. But no, Sleuth B was
quite certain ; certain of the man, the assumed name,
everything. Yes. It was this same " Richard

Mallard " who had landed at Southampton, who had put off the Home Secretary and Lord Delisport, whom he had shepherded up here and had duly delivered to his employer. There could be no doubt—and Worsing was almost reassured.

By ill-luck at that very moment Richard Mallard was telephoning to the station at Glasgow for a book he thought he had left behind in the train. The wires were crossed, and he caught phrases that perplexed him. . . . His own name in Worsing's voice, then in that of the Sleek and Smooth train acquaintance came something about Southampton. He heard the words : " He landed at Southampton." That was all. Could it be that here also was another of them ? But he had no proof, and he put the thought away.

All these days Sleuth A had remained discreet. He was content to know that his quarry was couched, not moving. He verified Mallard's presence at the hotel every morning from the boots and lay low.

Only once did Richard think he saw for a moment some figure in the yard which he vaguely seemed to have seen before—where was it ? In the Lakes ? But he soon forgot it. It had no significance for him : and when Sleuth B turned up in the afternoon Mallard greeted him warmly as an old friend.

Then it was that the blow fell, and for the third time there leapt abruptly into the young man's life that Horrid Affair.

On the evening of that day, after dinner, as they sat in the lounge, Worsing said quietly, " Mr. Mallard, do you think we might go up to my suite ? I'll have drinks sent up there. There's something I want to say to you in Private."

" By all means," said the younger man, fearing nothing. And up they went.

* * * *

Worsing was standing up, his elbow upon the mantelpiece, his fingers upon his forehead, staring at that coal fire which is the most comforting accompaniment to a Highland June.

" Mr. Mallard," he said slowly, " I don't want to press you if you would rather not tell me, but all these days I have been waiting to ask you, and hesitating to ask you, a simple question, the answer to which may make a great difference to my fortunes."

The uneasy Mallard said he would be delighted to be of service. Worsing turned his face round, looking at him directly and simply :

" To put it in a word, Mr. Mallard," he said, more

decisively, in a manner very different from the general fashion which had seemed natural to him since they had met, " may I hear from your own lips that you are empowered to deal with this Concession ? You can sell the interests or lease them ? I may deal directly with you."

Mallard groaned in spirit—Even here ! Even here in the Highlands and with this friendly old man the Evil Thing could arise suddenly and spring at him !

He had no idea it was near him. He had thought himself five hundred miles away from the torture and the browbeating and the spying and all the sickening consequences of those detestable " Mallard Millions." He was dazed at their sudden resurrection—and he sat silent.

Worsing repeated his question simple and slowly : " You are empowered to negotiate for the rights, Mr. Mallard ? "

Still more slowly the young man answered, with averted eyes and in a very low voice : " Yes ? Eh ! Why, I suppose so, sooner or later. What ? "

" It was all I wanted to know. Now I know that, I can await your convenience. I know you have been approached by others—but I believe you are still free ? "

" Oh, yes ! " replied the other uncomfortably.

" Well, Mallard," continued Worsing gently, looking down at him again in that straightforward, decisive fashion, " I don't want anything in writing yet, I will take your word for a beginning."

Richard Mallard became earnest, and clasped his hands over his knees, looked up at his companion as straightforwardly, he hoped, as he himself was being looked at, and said :

" Look here—frankly, Mr. Worsing, you know I can only tell you what I told the others. I must have time to consult with them at home. What ? To get details, anyhow. I really cannot act now—it wouldn't be honest, you know."

" No," said Worsing, turning his face away again to the fire, and drumming his fingers on the mantelpiece. " I quite agree, I quite understand. But perhaps we can make a beginning as I said. We are alone. I won't press you. Only I thought you could have told me, yes or no, for a foundation."

" Yes or no what ? " said Mallard.

" The concession—option if you like," said Worsing, immovable and still with his face turned to the fire. " If you'll consent to it in principle it'll be enough."

" But, you know, I've **nothing definite** to give," said

Mallard. " Upon my soul, I haven't anything definite enough. I could write, of course, or even cable. Oh, dear," he added with rising nervousness, " I'm sick and tired of the whole affair! It's the third time I've had to say that I really can't yet. It wouldn't be right. What? And after all I'm not sure it's worth anything. There's been such a lot of empty talk over it!" And he sighed.

There was a long silence.

" Well, Mallard," said the other, sighing in his turn and looking away again, " if you won't, you won't. But it would make matters much simpler; you know as well as I do it lies between me and them. One of us will satisfy you sooner or later, and I think I ought to tell you one thing; _we_—I, if you like: our group—could make it worth your people's while and your own, and more worth your while and theirs than anybody else can—even the Government. There are great and solid interests behind my offer, Mr. Mallard."

" What do you mean by worth my — their— while? Eh? I mean "—stammered Mallard.

" I mean," said Worsing, turning right round again, and this time putting both his hands behind him at the level upon the mantelpiece, the left hand far out to the left and the right hand far out

to the right, in a sort of deliberate tensity as of a
man who is determined to conclude, "I mean
that I want to bring things to an issue. An annual
rental of more than you could get if you exploited
it yourself : a concession for not more than thirty-
five years, and for yourself what you may think
just, whether in shares or cash. On the day we
understand each other I'm prepared to make a
preliminary payment, purely private and personal,
of fifty thousand pounds, or the equivalent in shares
when we float. I am authorised to do so."

And he was, for he had authorised himself.

It was the first time that any definite sum of
money, let alone fifty thousand pounds, had been
mentioned, and Richard Mallard was aghast.

He was not too well off, he could do with an
ampler income. He had had no hunger for money
hitherto. But the mention of money makes all men
prick up their ears. It was possible that in some way—
somehow—there might be an honest deal. But fifty
thousand pounds! And only for a sort of earnest money
or—well, *present*. To be straightforward—what ?

Of business hitherto he had known nothing, and
cared less ; his dividends were paid in, and that
was enough for him. And now this enormous lump
of gold fell like a thunderbolt into his simple life.

But how on earth could the phantom El Plantano claim be worth 50,000 pounds ? What was up ? Eh ?

He answered cautiously.

" It's a very large offer, you know, Mr. Worsing ! What ? "

" It is," said Worsing quietly. " But I mean it. I am fully authorised to make it. And remember this is for the personal payment only; the preliminary payment. What I sincerely think is due from us to you. And if you will take my advice you will make it shares—or perhaps " (he thought he saw something doubtful in Mallard's downcast face, and added hurriedly) " in part cash down and part shares. Oh ! " he continued, warming to his work, as he always did when really great affairs were in hand, " Surely you know that the possibilities are infinite ! When I think of all that it means . . . Yes, indeed, you would be wiser to consider shares. There's no end to what it may mean," and the old man came as near to enthusiasm as such can come. " And we're *right*, too," he continued emphatically—and quite truthfully. " If you will excuse my saying it, we who have handled such things for twenty years, and I myself, who have been dealing with them since I was quite a young man, would probably bring it to a better conclusion

than anybody else. If you would rather not have
a personal payment, but arrange, say, for a private
arrangement with your people at home we could
meet you. If you are authorised to offer the whole
thing for cash, at a much higher rate, instead of an
annual rental, we could meet you. We could arrange
a loan in New York and London. The only reason
I used the words ' personal payment ' was that I
wanted you to be quite clear that I thought it just
to you. For it's on you that our success depends."

" I see," said Mallard musingly, though he saw no
more than a blind man in a dark tunnel at night.

" Well, you can put it as you will," concluded
Worsing, " and as this is only a preliminary
conversation, I shall be quite satisfied if you tell
me that in principle you and those for whom you
are acting are agreed, say, upon an option alone."

" I don't see how I can accept here and now,"
began Mallard slowly, shaking his head. " I must
be clear as to what it may be really worth—I never
believed it worth the sum you mention for me
alone, let alone for the whole flotation."

" Mr. Mallard," broke in Mr. Worsing suddenly,
" it is unusual, I know, and perhaps you will be
offended. But may I tell you here and now, engaging
no one but myself, without any acknowledgment

passing, I am prepared to sign a cheque—here and now—for ten per cent. of the Personal Payment, for five thousand pounds. It's only ten per cent., and I must apologise ; but it will establish a record. And if you will allow me to say so, I trust you. If you accept there's no legal bond. But I shall believe that we will be the ultimate lessees."

Richard Mallard was at a stand.

" It engages me," he said.

" It will engage you to nothing," answered Worsing. " I don't know your movements ; I haven't even asked to see your credentials ; I leave for my house in the country to-morrow morning, and what you may be doing next I don't know. But I am in a position to sign that cheque, and I'll sign it. I may tell you frankly that money was put aside for that purpose—so keen are we upon this going through. You will find the cheque honoured and the sum paid into your account within four days ; they will take sixpence off, of course, for a Scotch cheque, for I shall draw upon our Glasgow bank. Now, shall we take it or leave it ? "

Richard Mallard came out well.

" You know, Mr. Worsing," he said, " for I've told you so twice, that I have been approached by more than one person already about this ? "

15

Worsing nodded.

" And I have told them all the same thing, what ? . . . . I don't think it fair to take anything—as yet. You know, I honestly don't think the thing's worth anything, what ? And even if it was, you know, I'd have to get details first. Honestly that's how I look at it. Honestly . . .! " And he shuffled uneasily.

Angus Worsing watched him steadily and fixedly beneath the bony arch of his brows. He was in two minds. Was this the blatant innocence it appeared to be ? He almost thought it was. Or was it the art of the actor ?

Happily for him, Angus Worsing knew little about art. He hadn't even heard the jargon of it ; so he stuck in two minds. Nevertheless, being of the blood and of the religion he was, he remained cautious. After a pause he said :

" Very well, Mr. Mallard, I respect your decision."

He stood silent for a good half minute, looking like a Raeburn portrait. Then he spoke, in those deep, careful tones :

" We've been very good friends Mr. Mallard, and I hope we shall remain so."

Richard Mallard had grown fond of the man in their brief acquaintance, and he said, " I hope so too, you know." Angus Worsing was the first of them to have dealt with him directly and manfully, and his timidity was reassured.

" That's right, Mr. Mallard . . . To-morrow I'm for my house as I said, Glenaber. It's a good house, though a new one. Will you not come with me there, and stay with me a few days? He paused. You'll find a good few of younger folks —and . . . and I'll promise not to say a word of business there. Only remember, my offer stands, and I'm free to open our conversation again if or when you have the full information."

Richard Mallard accepted, trusting in that promise to hear no more of the abominable thing, and next day in that fine car, accompanied by the smooth, the sleek, the demure, who was clearly an intimate friend, they rolled off to Glenaber.

* * * *

And to a grim little Granite Pub at the gates of Glenaber proceeded by public charabanc that very day Sleuth A. Nor was he alone. For believe me (incredulous reader) Sleuth C and Sleuth D were even now making their various ways North with speed from London to that same remote domain, and were due to reach it by evening.

CHAPTER VIII

THE Bishop of Shoreham has well remarked in his *Musings and Meditations* that one of the reasons everything is better done here than in foreign countries is the habit of leisure common to all classes of the community. "In every rank from Peer to Pauper" (such are his lordship's eloquent words) "the hours devoted to toil are strictly limited, those allotted to recreation are enlarged. Frequent and prolonged holidays are a universal rule. Therefore it is that we accomplish our tasks with a vivacity and precision that are the despair of our rivals."

It was four days after Richard Mallard's departure for the Lakes. Mary Bullar, Prime Minister of England, Scotland and Wales (but no longer Ireland), was going through her list, with Delavere in attendance, in her room at the House of Commons.

Mallard had gone off on Thursday morning. This was Monday afternoon, at the useful hour of three. Time to get through the list before Questions. The

Thursday itself had been Cup Day at Ascot, when one couldn't expect people to be in time, and Friday, of course, everyone goes away for the week-end. Mary Bullar had been with the Mastons—and that's four hours from Town : Delavere at his cousin's in Surrey, but knowing the hour of his chief's return, and therefore in no hurry.

Towards the end of the list was the starred word "Irania." Yes! By the way! Mary Bullar remembered.

"You've seen that fellow who calls himself Mallard again ? "

"Not since I told you about it last."

"Let me see, that was Wednesday—my word! Nothing since Wednesday ? "

"I was wanting to see you. But he's sure to be at the Titanic, or they'll know there. I'll get on to them."

He got on to them,—it took a minute or two and Mary Bullar was getting up steam.

"The Titanic ? Yes, the Prime Minister's Secretary speaking. Can you tell me if Mr. Mallard is still in the hotel ? . . . No, *Mallard* . . . No, Mr. Richard *Mallard*—M for Mabel . . ."

"Here ! Give it me ! " said his Chief rather too loudly. "The Titanic ? The Prime Minister speaking."

The other end of the wire went down on its stomach, for it was but a menial. " Yes, that's the name . . . Richard Mallard . . . Left London last Thursday morning ? Where for ? . . . Nonsense ! He must have got a ticket . . . All right, I'll hold on."

She held on, and her pressure increased. Delavere was perturbed. He felt his stock was falling.

" Billy, you're a fool ! " commented Mrs. Bullar by way of filling up the time. Then the telephone talked again and she listened with puckered brow. " The Lakes ? That's no address . . . Reserved a seat as far as Lancaster . . . Damn ! "

She crashed the receiver back on to its hook, and turned to poor Delavere : he ventured a word. " The Home Office will be sure to have him on a string."

" Go over to the Department *now* and see what they've done about it."

He ran over to the Department to find out what they had done about it. They had done nothing about it. They said : " You see, Thursday was Ascot, and then . . ."

Delavere raced back, just as the House met for Questions.

There was no time to be lost. The Home Secretary

passed a dreadful ten minutes with his angry cousin. The Department was stirred up, messages began passing out to a score of stations, and actually within two hours the Home Office had their man going northward.

It would be treason to give you his name. Hence do I label him no more than Sleuth C. But I'll tell you this much : he was known at the Yard as Sandy Jim. He had originally been marked for the Profession, of course, by his talent for hiding his social origins (a Sergent), but he got this particular job by being first on the list, as is the official way.

He was a lanky, forbidding sort of cove, dreadfully thin, and with the one merit of being uncommunicative. He'd have done for an ostler, and his motto was slow but sure. In about a week, after a thorough exploration of South-East Cumberland, he picked up his clue, and reported " The Clan Tarroch Hotel." Then he had a good night's rest, a comfortable breakfast, took the train, reported from the Clan Tarroch Hotel next day " Glenaber Castle," and went at his ease to draw the neighbourhood of that majestic pile for lodgings. He got them at the grim little Granite Pub which already sheltered Sleuth A, who sized him up as he came into the bar. Lord Delisport's

Sleuth A as he sized up the Home Office Sleuth C had the artist's contempt for the official : the historian's for the don : the living spirit for the machine. As for Sleuth C, he did all the regular things in exact routine. He made friends with a groom over a drink. He drew up a list of the guests at the Castle. He walked all the way to Inverary and telephoned at length to his Department the interesting information that Richard Mallard was still at Glenaber and that nothing was yet known about his future movements.

Far off in London the masterly intellect of Lady Caroline Balcombe had been tardily seized of the situation. She had been full of greater things in her own Department during those days ; there had been the very difficult affair with Italy over the Cingalese rebate (happily settled), the American claims over the Wakahanna incident (unhappily settled), and the eternal Singapore Condominium —not settled at all. She had taken it for granted that the Home Secretary—or his more competent staff—had kept contact with the Envoy, she knew that the negotiations were delicate, apparently they had been prolonged. Well, there was nothing to be astonished at in that. But one day she casually asked of Callingham how things were going in that

Sleuth C : being the Detective specially chosen by the Home Office for no particular reason

business. Callingham had referred to the Home
Office, and so did it reach the stupefied ears of Lady
Caroline that they had let their man bolt, lost
sight of him for days, only sent an Agent to track
him after an incredible delay, and were now still
seeking him.

She lost not a moment. She tackled her miserable
colleague, Harry Hardham, and made him suffer
as he had not suffered even at the cousinly hands
of Mary Bullar.

" Where's your Mallard ? " she said.

The Home Secretary used dignity. " We have
ample news of Mr. Richard Mallard, Carrie," he
answered. " We have the services of a first-rate
man ; in fact, a man who, when I consider the
various qualifications which . . ."

" Where is he ? " sharply interrogated Caroline.

" We have full news of him only this morning,"
rejoined Hopeless Harry with hauteur—feeling that
he was scoring. " He is one of a House Party which
gathers this very afternoon at Glenaber Castle."

" Glenaber ! " shrieked Caroline. " That's
Worsing ! "

" Well ? " he asked.

" You contemptible idiot, don't you know what
Delisport and Worsing mean ? "

" I will *not* be called a contemptible idiot, Caroline. I *am* acquainted, I am proud to say, with Lord Delisport—and I am not one of those who despise him for his humble origin. Mr. Worsing I have never met, but I respect him for a great man of affairs, who . . ."

"Oh! Dry up!" shot forth the exasperated soprano voice, high in its octave. "Good God! Worsing may have nobbled him already! It's a matter of hours! Minutes! I must . . ." and in a flash she was at the telephone sending an order, then racing for her office, and within the quarter of an hour pouring out instructions to—but I must introduce Sleuth D.

Sleuth D (for Reasons of State I must not divulge his real name) was one of Caroline Balcombe's many triumphs, and among the greatest.

She had chosen him herself, personally, years before when she was still Under-Secretary, and he had proved himself all she could have desired.

She had first discovered him in the service of the late Charles Q. Banneken, the Copra King of Homer, Mo., earning a princely salary. She learnt his successes. She didn't hesitate to draw upon the Exchequer (under the heading of Office Furniture, Stationery and Sundries) a still larger salary which tempted this great Englishman (for he was born in Bungay, the brother and secretary of a distinguished Baptist Minister in that town) to return to his native country and to put his unrivalled genius at the disposal of the Empire.

He never failed. In the character of Henry Baker, millionaire owner of the yacht *Susan*, he had entertained Carramba aboard and had learnt and transmitted the design against the Azores. As a longshoreman (locally Tarry Tim), he had heard by night, concealed in a shelter, the whispered Branagan plot discussed on Brighton beach. As the burly and popular tenant for a season of Woolborough House in Grosvenor Street he had discovered, during a ball of princely magnificence the whole Hungerford incident, and had put the Government in a position to forestall that terrible conspiracy. As a retired Captain of the Mercantile Marine in Liverpool he had caused the arrest of the Annihilationist Agent at the very moment when he was taking ship with the secret plans of the new *Puffin* class upon his person.

Such was the man who, forty minutes after leaving Lady Caroline's presence, was tearing past Willesden in the Glasgow express, and next morning entered, fresh and hearty, the little Granite Pub at Glenaber.

*Sleuth D : being the Private Detective specially chosen
by Lady Caroline Balcombe in person for his
disarming joviality*

From an inner room, where he was breakfasting in silence with Sleuth A, Sleuth C. the lanky, the taciturn, heard that cheery voice and was glad. The sublime heads of the two Departments might be at loggerheads, but their subordinates were friends as well as colleagues, and the respect paid in the Profession to Sleuth D's exceptional earnings, coupled with his famous achievements, made them all proud to know him.

"Is that you?" openly cried Sleuth C, conscientious employé of the Department, as the great man entered, all jollity and go.

"What! You here?" came the breezy voice of the famous colleague from Another Department, and they shook hands warmly, while Sleuth A rose and bowed with a grace which, for once, belied his disreputable exterior and betrayed his Social Origin. There was not a Sleuth in Sleuthdom but revered the glorious and opulent Head of the Profession.

"Well, here we are all met together!" merrily condescended Sleuth D as he sat him down to the breakfast, "and I take it we all know each other and what we're all after? Eh? Never mind, mum's the word and each on his own." He turned to Sleuth A gallantly. "Your duty too, sir, no doubt! And I won't surmise, at least I won't say, whom it

may be *for*. That's each our own look-out, isn't it ?
We'll ask no questions and we'll be told no lies, eh ? "
And he laughed a reassuring laugh, while they
murmured their thanks.

" Each does his duty, gentlemen, and we're all
agreed ; and we know the rules, gentlemen, we know
the rules."

Very honourably were those rules kept, as they
always are.

Each found his own Avenue of Approach. Sleuth A
a poor little Tweenie at the Castle for whom Blind
Eros had made him a hero of romance ; Sleuth C
his accustomed groom, both indirectly learning
what passed at table ; Sleuth D more directly, for
with the daring of all great Captains he had gone
right for the central keep and was free of the Butler
himself at a price which neither of the others could
command.

As a matter of Precedence Sleuth D had the first
right to the telephone when they all went over
together to Inverary—moreover, it was Sleuth D
who paid for the Daily Car. But with fine punctilio
he yielded his place to Sleuth C, as having official
right, being of the Home Office. For that Department was the proper one to conduct National
Investigation. After him Sleuth D would take the

box. Last of all, and contented to be so, came Sleuth A.

Thus did my Lord Delisport, the Home Office and Lady Caroline Balcombe in person receive, in various degrees of detail, their information on the Sleuths' Progress and the doings and sayings of the Secret Agent for West Irania : How, apparently, Worsing had concluded nothing; how Worsing's Agent, the sleek, the smooth, the demure, was one of the house party in the same old Character of Liverpool Merchant; how the other guests were such (to the matter) unimportant names as Lord Arthur Barry, Mr. and Mis. Cavel, Sir Percy Bates, Miss Goff and old Mrs. Baddenham. One point Counted. Mallard's next place was Stratford-on-Avon. That was the Stratford of the many Stratfords, and it was duly noted down. It seemed a good ruse. What more natural than that an innocent tourist should burn to visit the tomb of the Bard ? Other Mutts had done so before him, others would do so after him. And what better place to disarm suspicion and to provide a secure meeting-place with someone of the Revolutionary Brethren or some Negotiator for a Foreign Power.

All was mobilised for Stratford-on-Avon. Thither would Sleuth A, Sleuth C, Sleuth D (so each assured each his own employer) follow in the very same train, and of that town were the police warned by the Home Office for action and instructions minutely prepared. The arrival of the Wanted One would be from the North. There was a careful description given and particular note was to be taken of the name under which he should register at the hotel, for he might well take another alias. Full information was at once to be telephoned to London. They would almost certainly be advised in good time of the train he had taken, and Sandy Jim would be on it. They must look out for him.

* * * *

Richard Mallard in those few days of large hospitality began—once more!—to recover his composure. Worsing had been as good as his word. Not a syllable on the Tabooed Business, and it was fading rapidly from the young fellow's mind. He had even grown familiar with the presence of the smooth, the sleek, the demure, and was ready to accept him at face value and to dismiss those suspicions which had troubled him at the Clan Tarroch. It is hard to spend many days in quiet company and still believe it hostile.

On the third day a trifle, for a moment, disturbed him.

16

He was walking with his host on the high road,
coming back by a round after a stroll together
to the ruins of the original castle, a mile away.
On that high road, not far from the South Lodge of
Glenaber was a little Granite Pub, and outside it
a bench. On that bench, sunning themselves in the
fine summer weather, were three men sitting and
talking. One might be a sea captain, a large hearty
figure, the most conspicuous. The second was a
very thin, lanky, dismal sort, bony-faced. It was
the third that intrigued him. He could have sworn
it was that bar lounger who had looked into the
" Black Horse " in the Lakes and of whom he thought
to have caught a glimpse at the Clan Tarroch.

When two men walk together on an empty road
past an inn and three others sit idle at the doors
thereof surveying the highway, it is inevitable that
these should look up at those passing by. It is an
unconscious gesture which all make. None of the
three made it. They all looked away together, and
the effect was strange.

He was still under the influence of that coincidence
—or worse—when, the next day, a new guest
coming to Glenaber added to his ill-ease and made
it poignant.

She was familiar to those who know the wealthy

through newspapers alone as the Honourable
Arabella Burnett, to the registers in Somerset
House as Arabella Jane St. Valery Slackett,
born in 1944, spinster, but to her equals as Balmy
Jane.

Her appearance supported the epithet. Her pale
and scanty hair was commonly at random, her very
light grey eyes, though weak, betrayed strange
enthusiasms, and her gestures could be too emphatic.

She was a Redeemer of the Human Race and a
Redresser of Wrongs—in theory and as literature.

But she made her rounds of visits as they all do
in that world, for the family was a great one and
she was related to half the others. Corvan had
married her sister, Sir Henry Hardham was her
uncle, Mary Bullar, therefore, her mother's cousin.

She was of the Brethren, she held Annihilationist
views. She suffered for the sufferings of man.
She knew that light had come from the East, that
salvation had appeared in Moscow more than sixty
years ago, and that now the dawn had spread over
the East. Though still wickedly resisted in Europe,
Asia had felt the thrill, and no district had played
a greater part in this Liberation of Mankind than
West Irania, and no one in West Irania had used
more burning words than the Agent who was now

in England. How splendidly he had denounced
the atrocities at Pangbar! How nobly he had
laboured for the emancipation of mankind.

For she knew of his arrival and of what was
passing. She was of those few hundreds who hear
something of what is really happening, and no
one minded her hearing; for if the middle classes
regarded her with a mixture of awe for her rank and
of horror at her speeches, her own lot knew her to
be harmless. It is rather chic to have a few reds
knocking about. They season the dish.

She knew, not only that they were hunting him for
the Concession, but that there was the alternative of
arrest; the danger thrilled her! How she envied
her sister, Lady Corvan, for having been privileged
to entertain him at her own table! How she burned
to help!

With what a leaping heart, then, did she hear
that name at her first introduction—Mallard! It
was the name under which her Divinity had chosen
to disguise himself, and as she looked at the gentle
face, the quiet eyes, she was indignant at the way
Capitalism had maligned him. She had been firmly
sure that all those tales of the tortures, and the
drownings in the Caspian, were lies. Now she was
trebly sure. Her hand shook as it touched his own

and as she heard a melodious voice murmuring, with the slightest of foreign accents :

" I've, I've never had the pleasure, you know, I mean to say, what ? "

As for him, he was uncomfortably aware of two pale eyes lit with a new fire. He faintly blushed.

But it was only a beginning. She manœuvred to sit next him at dinner and poured out her wealth of indignation against the grievous inequalities of the world. She took for granted—her voice trembling with praise—his having something to do, for or against, something called the Pangbar atrocities. She occupied him like a conquered country.

After dinner she had no opportunity to speak to him more than a few words, but she followed him continually with her looks—to the no small amusement of Sally Goff, to the indignation of old Mrs. Baddenham, Worsing's sister, who was acting as hostess.

Her chance came again next morning at breakfast. There were only four down, and the two others were talking loudly together. She drew her chair near Mallard's, and, just as he was conveying a bit of sausage to his mouth, she said hurriedly in low tones :

" You are in peril ! "

He dropped the sausage and his teeth met on nothing.

" Eh ?   What ? "

" You are in peril !" said the low voice again, and he felt a hand laid discreetly under the table on his arm.

He was horribly frightened. But just at that moment Worsing came, giving him good morning strongly, and he was for the moment saved.

But not for long. For less than an hour.

At the low words of Arabella Slackett all the turmoil in him had re-arisen. His soul was seething. He felt trapped. He sought the garden alone to calm himself in the silence and the scented air under the great trees, when in a secluded place where thick laurels intervened between him and the house he heard a voice behind him and started in alarm. He had come to know it too well in those few hours. There was a blow to come.

He was handed it by the Honourable Arabella Slackett.

She came up suddenly, pushing her way through the dense laurels, like a far from developed Diana at the chase, she faced him in all the sunny girlishness of her thirty-five years, and fixed him with her gaze.

Richard Mallard was rooted. He was held. He

*Petrifying effect of Balmy Jane upon
Mr. Richard Mallard*

didn't even continue his original twist and start.
He froze on it. But within he was all protest. Was
it not enough that he had endured her at breakfast?
That he had been compelled the last night to hear
flaming whispers on the Pangbar atrocities? Was
it not enough that he had been condemned to
answer something, anything, anyhow, to all that
horrible diatribe against the poor or the rich—he
had really forgotten which it was? Must he suffer
more? Why had this female fiend sought him out
for a special victim? What had *he* done? There
were lots of other men in the house who could
stand it better than he could; men more like heaps
of turf, or tortoises. He had no strength to repel
such attacks. Therefore did he stand transfixed.

But his mood in no way discomposed her. She
was the Wrath of God. And even as he braced
himself to receive the first discharge of the Pangbar
atrocities, he discovered how much worse was in
store for him. For the jejune but resolute Arabella
fell suddenly at his astonished feet, clasped her
hands, and cried to him, gazing upwards in a
Messianic ecstasy, "Saviour! Deliverer!"

As she thus looked up into his face the panic
thereon depicted affected her not at all. Her faith
saw the true man behind such a mask. Her eyes

*Immoderate gesture of Balmy Jane under the influence
of Democratic enthusiasm*

would have filled with tears had she been able to summon them. As it was, they glowed with the ecstasy of vision.

" We are alone ! " she whispered. (It was abominably true !) She rose suddenly to her feet, and looked fully at him with her full, excessive vision.

" You fear nothing ? " she half whispered intensely. " You know that I will never betray you ? Saviour ! Deliverer ! I will save you in your turn ! "

" Eh ? What ? " gasped the unfortunate man.

" Be confident," she answered, heaving. And again she added, heaving : " We are alone."

With an advance closely recalling Ethel Napier in the part of Lady Macbeth sleep-walking, she approached him.

" You are in peril ! " she breathed. " You are in mortal peril—but your salvation is near. At my hands ! "

She extended them towards him. Her face neared his own. For a dreadful second he feared her lips—she expected his. But the Hero of Human Liberation lacked initiative. The spell broke, and he ran like a hare for the house. Balmy Jane had missed her tide.

* * * *

In his room, a hunted hare taking refuge, Richard

Mallard trembled. He felt in confused mixture some dreadful fate of which he had been warned, a lunatic woman threatening he knew not what, spies left and right—and, in such a mood, he stiffened again and stood rigid with open eyes at hearing two phrases under his window. The first was Worsing's :

" Never lose contact. Follow him when he leaves and report everything."

The second — oh ! Conscious heart ! Oh ! Prescient terror—it was, it was indeed the voice of the Smooth, the Sleek, the Demure ; and it was answering.

" I shan't let him out of my sight." That was the breaking-point.

Richard Mallard fled, hat in hand, down the avenue, raced past the gates. He knew where the station was and ran for it blindly, instinctively, as good as mad.

He had a blurred impression as he tore down the road of three men coming on him from his right and running too, but his legs were long and he had the advantage of frenzy. Their hammering steps followed but grew fainter. A train whistled from up the glen. He put out all his powers, dashed just in time for his ticket and leapt in even as it moved out along the platform. Intuitively he had shouted "Glasgow" and left a little mountain of change.

He leant back in the railway carriage panting, hardly knowing what he had done—but free.

Into the station, sweating and gasping, first Sleuth A, then Sleuth C, and, apoplectic, the exhausted massiveness of Sleuth D successively stumbled. Immediately after came a whistling rush, and there whisked round and halted with a grinding of brakes a car which Worsing himself drove, hatless, blazing; beside him the Sleek, the Smooth, the Demure, no longer Sleek but sweating, no longer Smooth but ruffled up, no longer Demure but at bursting-point, leapt to the ground.

They were too late. Their violent gestures were unheeded. The express was but a rapidly lessening roar down the glen, and Worsing cursed himself to remember that it was he who had paid his own good money to have it halted at the little place, with no stop before Glasgow. And motors were no use! Oh! It was a good train!

*   *   *   *

In the train Richard recovered. He remembered. He'd left his things behind. He'd played the lunatic—but he was free . . . What a moment!

He took out his ticket—it was for Glasgow only. He felt for his money and his traveller's checks. They were on him. Good! Well, he'd go on at once to find his main luggage in London at the Titanic, the rest could slide. He'd sleep on it and decide what to do. Anyhow, he was out of one net. Sufficient unto the day. But the cloud was heavy on his mind, for he'd been driven to extremes and nothing was secure.

He reached the Titanic the next morning, gave no explanation of his lack of hand-bags, secured a room and had his main luggage brought up to him that he might change and face the world . . . and his advent was duly reported.

It was reported, as was but right, to the man who had paid most money, to Lord Delisport The rest could wait. If the Home Office wanted information they could always ask for it. They were only a nuisance, anyhow, more trouble to the hotel than they were worth, and never anything for the porter : and, after all, it was the porter who sent the news.

*   *   *   *

Those donkeys who tell us that great fortunes are made by luck rather than brains would change

what minds they have if they could see the first
Marquis of Delisport acting on the message from
the Titanic.

He opened his diary to verify the exact words
from the North, received yesterday. Mallard had
fled—fled, leaving his luggage. Why? There
could be only one reason. Something urgent
telephoned from Stratford-on-Avon, something
imperative. Mallard was at the Titanic? He must
have got this Stratford fellow to come up, or to
meet him on the line.

Had anything been clinched with Worsing? Or
with the unknown Stratford man? He couldn't
tell. But the essential thing was to get hold
of Mallard—once he had hold of Mallard he had
a plan.

And how could he get hold of Mallard? Mallard
was not to be got hold of by the prospect of
negotiation—that had failed.

He had an idea.

He rang up the Titanic—he wondered whether
he should have the luck. He had the luck. Richard
Mallard himself answered the telephone.

" Look 'ere, Mr. Mallud, I'm Lord Delisport
'imself torkin'. No sekertary, mind yer, just Lord
Delisport hisself. You tike me, don't yer ? "

The telephone answered " Yes "—doubtfully.

" I've got good news fer yer. Straight I 'ave ! "

The telephone didn't answer. It was thinking a lot of things in a whirl.

" News as'll relieve yer greatly. I'm glad to have the giving of it . . . Naw ! Naw ! Nothin' to do with that ol' stiff. Ferget it ! Mr. Mallud ! Burn it up ! Jes somethin' yer'll find ter be very good news indeed."

The telephone was wavering.

" Wall, I admit it's short notice. *Sharp* notice, in a manner o' speakin'. *Could* yer come round this evenin'. Naow, look 'ere " (in an ecstasy of condescension), " could yer come an' *dine ?* If yer can't do that, yer might come round after, say about ten . . . Oh, yer could ? Well, come and dine, like a good feller. I want to tork to yer private· So long. 8.30 we call it."

So simple are the traps for catching pigeons. But not everyone can (or will) set them.

*   *   *   *

The dinner at Lord Delisport's was of no particular moment ; it was of such a sort as you might find in the house of any great English peer of to-day, or at least of any great English peer connected with the commercial side of Imperial affairs. There were but fifteen guests, all men : two of them politicians ; one of them a professor, another of the sort that play bridge in rotation from house to house ; two with ancient names, a blackmailer or so, and the rest I know not who.

Richard Mallard was kept until the last of them had escaped. As a rule those who enjoyed the hospitality of that famous roof were pressed to stay, often against their desires; but to-night it was not so. It seemed as though Lord Delisport desired to be alone. And so he did—but alone with Richard Mallard.

When they were so alone, Lord Delisport led him upstairs to his study, and Richard Mallard awaited with some eagerness the piece of good news. He came straight to the point, as it was his pride to do.

" Look 'ere, Mr. Mallud," he said, " afore we tork o' this bit o' good news, I've got a bone to pick with you."

" What's that ? Eh ? " said Richard, standing off a little at the tone. But there was more than the tone to come. Lord Delisport lurched forward and poked the young man in the ribs, and added greasily :

" A bone about Scotland—understand ? "

" No, Lord Delisport. . . . I'm . . . I'm
afraid I don't understand. Hadn't you better
tell me what you said you would ? What ? It's
getting late, you know."

" What I said I would ? Well, it's good news,
but first I want ter arsk about Scotland."

Richard Mallard was getting nervous.

He got up as though he thought of going. The
interview had not lasted long, but it had lasted long
enough. If he was in for another bout of mystery
it was more than he could bear.

" I don't understand," he said. " I—d'you know—
don't quite understand why you asked me to dinner
at this short notice. And . . . And . . . I don't
understand why you don't tell me what you said
you would. Eh ? "

" Yer don't ? Wall, sit down," said Lord Delisport.
" Sit down. You young 'uns are so restive. No
offence meant. You know that, don't yer ? Lor'
bless yer, no one ever takes offence at me ! I may
be familiar ; I don't pretend I 'm not—using the
word in the same spirit as what it's meant—I mean
familiar in friendship, as Shakespeare says. Wot
call 'ave yer got to get your dander up ? I'm only
askin' yer about this Scotch affair." And he winked.
" We can do business."

17

The great leaders of English society are not without
energy, or they could not reach the summits they
do. Elderly though he was, the worthy peer heaved
himself up by the arm of his chair, looked straight
into the young man's eyes, and pressed him down
again by the shoulders.

" 'Ere now, sit down and 'ave a good talk abaht
it. Ye've been in Scotland, ain't yer ? " And he
winked again.

Whether Richard Mallard would have done well
to break out of the place at once and have done
with it all he does not himself know. But he sat
down again, resigned for the moment, and rather
bewildered.

" Well, you know—what is it ? " he said
tremulously.

Lord Delisport leaned back in the deep arm-chair
and for once spoke his inmost mind.

" Arrh ! You're a downy one ! " he gurgled.

There was genuine admiration in his tone, and
once more he winked, and once more his right hand
made as though to dig his companion in the ribs.
But he wisely forbore. " This Scotch business,"
he went on, half an octave lower. " Think I don't
know all abaht it ? *D'yer think I never 'eard the
name o' Worsing ?* D'yer think " (raising his tones)

"Angy Worsin' and I 'aven't been neck and neck, and pals, and yet not pals, if yer gets me, in a manner of speakin', this twenty years ? Lor' bless me . . ."

" Lord Delisport," broke in the unfortunate Mallard, in a quavering voice, " for Heaven's sake let us stop this—eh ? I mean, you know, I don't know what you mean by all this going to Scotland ; I don't know what you mean about Worsing."

But he was only told for the third time that he was a downy one ; and he found no issue. Before he could raise himself for a final exit Lord Delisport was leaning forward, emphasising the whole of what I have heard called his magnetic personality, with strong, bulging eyes, curls wagging on either side of his square head, and a fat, uplifted hand.

" Look 'ere," he said, " I'll do the fair thing by yer if yer'll stand by me. If yer don't stand by me—'struth, I'll *break* yer."

" Oh, all right," said Mallard, getting up now firmly and making for the door. " I'm sick and tired of this nonsense. What ? " He actually shouted that " what."

" Oh, you are, are yer ? " The great peer and captain of industry had hauled himself up again and was standing facing his opponent. " You are, are yer ? Well, now, perhaps yer don't know . . .

I'm goin' ter give yer that bit of good news," and he grinned.

" Let me go ! " shouted Mallard ; he dashed for the handle of the door of the little study and shook it. He was legitimately surprised to find that it was locked.

" Miss Gaylord," called Lord Delisport to the surrounding air, and a very discreet, very neatly dressed, very quiet young woman came out from behind a thick curtain which nobly draped one of the windows of the room. " Yer've got that all down, 'aven't yer ? "

" Yes, Lord Delisport," said the unmoved lady in a business-like tone.

" Read it to 'im," ordered the peer.

Miss Gaylord read ; and it was really astounding. Richard Mallard, it seemed, had in a few brief, well-chosen words, been driven to admit that he would give the concession to Lord Delisport's group. He had been approached by Mr. Worsing, during a recent visit to Scotland, and he had heard what offers the Government had seen fit to make ; but the matter was now settled as between him and Lord Delisport for (here followed the figures). He desired that a memorandum to that effect should be drawn up, and in due course he would sign it.

Excellent Business Ruse of Lord Delisport

"That's my good news," said the host—and he grinned.

There was a pause of perhaps thirty seconds—Richard Mallard standing up very white and angry ; Lord Delisport self-possessed, and Miss Gaylord still more self-possessed and perfectly at her ease.

"Will you let me out, or will you not ? " shouted Richard.

"I don't know what yer mean by letting yer out, Mallud," said Lord Delisport. "Yer could 'ave gone whenever yer chose." And sure enough, when Richard Mallard tried the handle of the door in a fury it opened easily enough.

"I shall remember this ! " he cried angrily over his shoulder. But that same shoulder his host tapped cheerfully as he followed him into the hall.

"Not afore the servants," he said quietly. "Not afore the servants —— " and then, louder, "Mr. Mallud wants a taxi, Johnson."

"Yes, m'lord," said Johnson, and sure enough a taxi was waiting.

With a set mouth and an expression as determined as his own unfortunate soul was in a whirl and staggered, Richard Mallard passed out, without a good night, and heard the taxi told to drive to his hotel.

For the moment, in his maze, he was about to give another address—the railway ; but he thought better of it. He sank back into the cab, and wondered whether he was awake or dreaming ; and when he reached the Titanic had occasion to wonder still more. For, in the brilliant light of the courtyard, he thought he recognised the driver's face.

He slept that night not at all. In the agony of it his mind clarified and his decision was made by morning. England was a mad-house for him. He must put the sea between him and all this Bedlam. He must cut himself off altogether.

CHAPTER IX

In the town of Stratford-on-Avon four wearied
men, exasperated by a night in the train and changes
at unearthly hours, foregathered in the lounge of
the Swan of Avon, the new and complete hotel
which mirrored its 12 stories in the Historic Stream.
They were restoring themselves with cock-tails,
and they were Sleuth A, Sleuth B, Sleuth C and
Sleuth D.

Common misery had made them friends and
opened their hearts all one to the others, though the
rigorous rules of the Profession were well maintained;
nobody poached and nobody cut in. Each served
faithfully for his pay.

But really it was very disappointing! They had
dragged Stratford like a horse-pond and not a sign.

They were having their last drag. The Swan of
Avon had told the Police that a young man who
might be the Wanted One had come that hour: by
name Tomkinson. But when the boy in buttons
had bawled " Tomkin*son* " at the top of his voice

through ten rooms, the yellow brute in horn
spectacles who appeared was as much like Richard
Mallard as Mary Bullar was like the Empress of
Abyssinia.

The telephone queries came raining in from
both Departments, from Lady Caroline herself,
from Worsing—oddly enough none from Lord
Delisport : that nobleman was holding his hand.
Quite late at night there came a call for Sleuth A.
It told him to come up by the first morning
train. The fox had gone to earth again in the
Titanic.

Sleuth A obeyed ; Sleuths B, C and D, finding
Sleuth A gone and finding it was for London, rang
up their masters to say that it looked like London.

The Home Office, Worsing, Delisport learnt from
the Titanic that their man had flitted by the boat
train—and the one to do the right thing was, as
you may imagine, Lady Caroline.

She got on to the Quai d'Orsay and deluged
them with particulars. Stop him at Boulogne !
Stop him anywhere ! It was urgent in their common
cause. If he had got away, had they, the French
Police, the right man to track him ?

They had. They had a man indistinguishable
from an Englishman, who would excite no suspicion

in the victim's breast.* One whose idiom was perfect, whose accent exact, whose clothes and hat and even boots were pure St. James's, and one, moreover, whose very manner was English: silent, reserved, gentleman. If he failed none could succeed. He would run the game down and hand it over without fail. By name Hippolyte Dubois. In the Profession Armand de Berensac.

With all that arranged, Caroline Balcombe and the Prime Minister arranged the sequel. When he was nabbed he was to be handed over to an English escort—they wouldn't call it police—and jugged: what for could be discussed later, if nothing cropped up they could always make it official secrets or something—there'd be plenty of evidence for *that*. The great thing was to nab him: after that he could be cooked to what sauce they pleased, and made easier to deal with.

* * * *

A man who has had no sleep at all will be bad at staff work. He will do disconcerting things.

But then, the man who is bad at staff work and does disconcerting things may well throw his pursuers off the scent. Richard Mallard got up

* *Attention is directed to the Frontispiece.*

more dead than alive on that fine late summer morning, took a taxi to Victoria and boarded the train for Folkestone. He was so distracted by the chase and harass of the last few days that he was ready for anything—braced to any peril, to any challenge.

There was no peril, there was no challenge. The man at the barrier at Victoria hardly opened the passport; the man who stamped it at Boulogne had, after the fashion of the Third Republic, received no information. The telephone message sent to the Quai d'Orsai at noon was still in process of being copied, re-copied, counter-copied, duplicated, recorded, filed, and then put into its carton, before they would worry the gentleman at Boulogne. Some time next week he might be advised.

Thus did Richard Mallard land unmolested upon the seeming hospitable shores of the Gaul.

Of the Continent he knew nothing. Of France, nothing. Of the French language, happily for him, so much as the somewhat cosmopolitan surroundings of Havana had rendered familiar, and the instruction of the underpaid French master at his school.

Richard Mallard had fixed upon no inn. He would take his chance. Upon one thing, at least, he was determined: that it should be in a village, and no town. With a cunning worthy of a better cause, a cunning of which he would have been incapable before the stropping and sharpening and honing and grinding of Fate had put an edge upon his tender wit, he decided to use some part of the slender store he had set aside in driving boldly through the country till he saw something he liked.

If he couldn't throw them off the scent that way, then there was no way of throwing them off the scent. And if he didn't throw them off the scent he would go mad.

He hired his taxi upon the Quay itself, and gave the driver the singular instruction to drive wherever he liked, so that it were far into the country, and he would tell him where to stop.

His French was indifferent, but as the driver was of the quiet Flemish race they understood each other, in spirit if not in words, as only two exiles can ; and the mild northerner at the wheel, who had suffered many things from the vivid intensity of the French, was drawn to the mild Mallardian face as to a brother's.

With wretched springs, on defunct cushions, Richard Mallard bumped over the countryside. He bumped for close on an hour, say twenty-two miles, when, at the entry to a small remote hamlet, where the road passed through a fine avenue of trees, he saw a house that appealed to him. It was of but two low stories. It was covered with creepers; it stood well back from the road; in the garden between it and the paling along the highway were somewhat rusty chairs and tables of iron, and there was painted along its front, " Au Jean Bart."

Who or what John Bart might be Richard Mallard could not tell. But that was the place for him. He paid the plaintive Fleming royally, and went in to the good hostelry as the storm-driven ship into harbour. Now, once and for all, was he his own master, and alone. He would forget the grave things he had suffered, the tortures beyond bearing; the dreadful nights, the ceaseless appearances of faces that knew him to the marrow, but of whom he knew nothing, save that they haunted him.

Alas! for the unarmoured soul! Alas! for those who, to-day, underestimate the powers of the modern State!

It was upon the second day of Richard Mallard's beatific repose that four gentlemen arrived in a taxi-cab. They also had come from Boulogne. The one had the aspect of an English public-house lounger; the other the aspect of a fairly well-to-do, sleek-haired man, mild and demure, as might be from the commercial classes of Liverpool ; the third was what people who have a poor vocabulary call hard-bitten, and threatened something at once Celtic and Calvinistic about his bony face ; the fourth was a hearty old sea-dog, well capable of shivering his timbers. All four had been playing nap under the instruction of the first, despite the alarming jolts of the road. All four invaded the Jean Bart, and Richard Mallard saw them as they came.

He was in an upper chamber. They had not seen him. He seized upon the advantage.

Have I not already made clear how misfortune can educate and how acute experience, to the very edge of agony, had developed the intelligence of Richard Mallard ? He lay down upon his bed, after ringing the bell. He told the landlady's daughter, who answered it, that he felt unwell and would sleep. The common eating-place of the inn knew him not that night.

With the first break of dawn, when the early rising French were already bustling about the place, he crept down with his small bag packed, and begged for the bill. They protested that he had given no notice, but money is the master of

all things, and a sufficient exaggeration in the way
of that kindness procured his escape.

Off he went, shuffling past with his bag in his
hand, up the street of the village, till, by good
fortune, he saw an early cart lumbering along the
road under the care of a sleepy driver. He begged
for a lift and tendered the all-conquering paper.
A lift was given him. In a mile or two they came
to a level crossing, with a tiny station-halt adjoining
it. Here Mallard got out, found that he had two
hours to wait for a train, waited the two hours, and
got in with a ticket to a place the name of which
had attracted him, because it was called, on the
time-table, " The High Seven Winds," " Les Hauts
Sept Vents."

But even as he steamed out he saw a two-
wheeled vehicle galloping furiously up, and he could
discern in the midst of their gesticulations four faces
which he ardently desired to be rid of for ever and
for ever and for ever.

He was too wise (by this time) to get out at the
High Seven Winds (which looked a miserable place,
anyhow). His taking of the ticket had left the
scent hot. He went on in the little trundle train
for another good hour, till he came to the station
of a pleasant-looking country town. Out he got,

paid his extra fare, and flattered himself that he had broken the scent for good.

. Poor Innocent ! Who can destroy record in the modern world ? Are there not tickets and receipts for tickets ? Is there not a carbon copy of everything ? And is not all the time in which we live like one huge haystack of document and document and document, wherein all that we do is set down ?

It is true that the Fatal Four had disappeared for some few days from his life. Even that respite he owed to nothing better than the interminable copying and recopying of the French police system. But the first information had already reached headquarters in Paris, and the redoubtable Hippolyte was on the march for the North.

All dispositions were taken. The staff work was of the best. At a summons the Gendarmerie would appear at any one of the fifty-three places marked very neatly in green ink upon a map of the Département after a close calculation of the radius wherein the fugitive might be found.

Of the fifty-three, twelve had been drawn ; the thirteenth was a find. Hippolyte shot a rapid glance at a little photograph hid in the palm of his hand, compared it with the gentle face which mildly

surveyed the market-place from the garden of the
cafe, and knew that he had hit the bull's-eye.

He went first of all to the police station and
presented his papers. There did he give his orders
—but for the morrow. He was proud of himself.
There never had been a better bit of stalking.

I say that Hippolyte was proud of himself. I
am sorry to say that Hippolyte was weak upon that
side. He was proud of himself upon too many
things. He was particularly proud of his English
accent, his English vocabulary, his manner
indistinguishable from an Englishman's. He had
registered under the simple name of Smith, giving
for his private address the comprehensive but
familiar name of London. At dinner he tackled the
Pursued One in his native tongue.

" The time is fine," he said. " It was but time.
We shall have beautiful time for some time. I
so hope all times. Is it not so ? "

A vague throb of fear passed through Richard
Mallard's soul, like the throb of an old wound.
There was something sinister about this.

But he put a good enough front on it.

" Parliament will have a meet again," continued
Hippolyte, whom we will call Sleuth E, and even,
in compliment to his nationality, E with an accent.

18

" When I am back at London I shall hope to hear debate. I am fond of the Chamber. You also ? "

So it went on. There was no topic concerned with the Ancient Mistress of the Seas which Hippolyte had not at his fingers' end. He had been at a Public School, the name of which he had suddenly forgotten ; he had business in Manchester, of which city he could name many citizens by their little names, so familiar was he with it all. And he asked who was chief of the gentleman's cricket equipment ; he had been so long away that he knew it not the least, alas !

On all these things did Hippolyte discourse, and with every phrase did Mallard grow more anxious and more reserved. It wouldn't do !

He felt it in his bones that all this was uncanny. None the less, he had to bear this persistent acquaintance and remained suspecting only till one small incident threw him back into the old panic.

It was a slip of paper which he found lying on a table, mis-laid with a couple of jotted notes in French. What the notes meant he could only half understand. They were composed of detailed French words, a dozen or so, and half of them technical. But one thing in them was unmistakable. He saw his own name written there very plain, and the hair of his head stood up.

It was a radiant late summer morning that the shock had fallen, and Richard Mallard felt indeed as though there were no friend left in this world, nor any refuge from that terrible machine, State and Capitalist, of which he had become a victim.

He awaited what Fate might send, and what Fate sent was, of course, her Darling Four.

They had started with a better scent than Hippolyte, for they had the ticket office to go by, and they only had to try the successive farther stations on the line till they found where excess had been paid ; but they got in after him, and Sleuth C had his C.I.D. card on him, and satisfied the local police in each place of his mission ; generously covering A and B with his mantle. As for D, *he* had the Mystery Sign and could go anywhere.

It was a couple of hours after finding the notes of Hippolyte that the Four were revealed. Richard Mallard was sitting at his little table in the front garden of the café, facing the square, when he was aware, under the awning of a café opposite, of a card party merrily at work, and it was unmistakable : there was the Burly Sea Dog, there the Sleek, the Smooth, the Demure, slowly discarding with thoughtful face, there the hard-bitten, bony face of Sandy Jim, and opposite him in the shadow, sizing up his hand, the intelligent degradation of Sleuth A. They had found him.

Not a glance did they turn in his direction, not a sign did they give of their triumph. But Mallard knew well that he was attacked. His mood turned to a sullen acceptation of the surveillance. But it was relieved by this thought, which singularly lightened his mind. They could report his place of refuge (they had already done so that morning), they could even arrange with this Frenchman (Sleuth C had shown Hippolyte his card an hour since, and Hippolyte, in a superior manner worthy of his rank and clothing, had returned the compliment) ; they could follow him—they presumably would—in his next move. But they could do nothing more. The only one he was supposed to know was Worsing's Sleek and Demure One, and that modest engineer had clearly made it a point not to barge in.

Richard Mallard made the best of it ; he might be watched ; it burdened his life, but it was not as though he were in England, where such watching led directly to cross-questions by Politicians, to Police Cells, to sudden flights across country, traps, conspiracies and sleepless nights. They wouldn't come over here to pester him, he supposed—not even Delisport. And if they did, they had no power.

In this mixture of relief and gloom he was approached by the Courteous Hippolyte, who came up to him garbed for the Promenade, and suggested that exercise.

"Perhaps would you, sir, make a walk."

Richard Mallard was in no mood for his companionship, and, being of English blood, he did not conceal his desire to be alone.

"Thank you. I don't feel much like walking, you know."

Hippolyte resented the tone like a blow. He had been courteous, even affable, and the young man had no right to be bearish. Hippolyte was not cruel. He had a duty to do, but he would do it as politely as possible, and he planned that they should be removed from the common gaze. Richard had refused. Moreover, Hippolyte had all the French acerbity ; his resentment had a keen edge and was dangerous. Nevertheless, he restrained himself.

He continued to be suave :

"Can it not be that we visit the walls ? " he said. "Which are of the most high interest. Also there is the Bishopric which I have known in the time."

This time Richard did not even answer. He only shook his head. It was bad enough to be spied upon. He didn't see why he should make sham friends with spies into the bargain. Who was employing Hippolyte he didn't know and hardly cared : probably Delisport. Anyhow, he was no fit companion.

For the third time Hippolyte returned to his task :

" No ? Then perhaps we sit here and chat a little, is it not ? "

Richard's disinclination for such an occupation was expressed by a rigid silence, and looking straight before him as though the Frenchman were not there.

Anger rose and raged, though still on the curb, within the mind of Hippolyte. Ah ! It was like that ! They would mock themselves of him ? We shall see !

" Would you be surprised . . . " he began in very cold, clear tones.

Richard Mallard answered with a sharp phrase, still looking straight before him.

" Nothing can surprise me any more," he said.

*Richard Mallard expressing his incapacity
for surprise*

But there he was wrong. The Agent of the French Police made a sign which Mallard never saw. He was still gazing before him with a deliberate sullen avoidance of the other's face, when he was startled out of his life to feel a large hand clapped from behind on either shoulder, and behold! two gigantic Gend'armes of an appalling appearance held him as Ogres might their prey. On Hippolyte's lips was a small, tense smile and his eyes glistened.

As they marched poor Mallard away he followed immediately behind like the chief mourner, and the devoted Four in the café opposite rose and fell in after, to complete the funeral procession.

*   *   *   *

On the boat, in a private cabin, Richard Mallard sat between two gentlemen in plain clothes who did not molest him, but who gave him to understand that they preferred his remaining where he was, and would, on landing, accompany him to London. The authorities had a carriage reserved. The prisoner—he supposed he was a prisoner—bore it as well as he could. He listened while they told him that they would submit him to no indignity, their orders were to see that he reached London in

*Discovery by Mr. Richard Mallard that he is
still capable of surprise*

their custody. There he would, of course, be under surveillance, but no one need know it, and he would be told where and when and by whom he would be wanted. Only, he must accompany them quietly and make no attempt to communicate with others or to leave them during the journey. For the rest, he was free to order what refreshments he chose, to smoke and to get the papers and all the rest of it. He was agreeable. There was nothing else to be done.

On the deck above, in God's fresh air, the Four, faster friends than ever, rejoiced in the termination of their various missions and common task. Their rewards were before them. Their work had been successfully accomplished, home was nearby, across a calm and sunlit sea. They had the right to indulge their happy mood.

But Hippolyte, who was charged with the duty of crossing until he should have exchanged papers at Folkestone, was not of their party. He knew his place. He was strict on the Protocol. It was his to carry out the orders of his superiors, and he was officially ignorant of all their actions, sure, indeed, that he was cognisant of Sandy Jim as being also official—but now obviously of inferior rank as to prevent any hobnobbing. Therefore

Irregular attitude of Sleuths A, B, C and D
towards Sleuth E (with an accent)

did Hippolyte stand apart, cautiously indeed, but apart.

It did not save him from the boyish humour of the Four. But he made no reply. It was an ordeal and must be borne. Only to this slight extent did he unbend, that when, at Folkestone, as he passed them on the quay to exchange his papers, he bowed to them with some ceremony and assured them that their conduct had been perfectly irregular.

*   *   *   *

It was evening, though still light, when the boat train reached Victoria, and Richard Mallard, tired, ill-resigned, but still unmolested, got out of the reserved compartment with his companions. He asked them if he might walk and send his bag on. He desperately wanted the air after all those hours of confinement. They hesitated a moment, but the one who had seemed to be in command from the first said at last that he saw no harm in it : only, of course, they must keep together. They went by the less crowded back streets and across St. James's Park towards the Archway, at the end of the Mall.

They had already passed under this and were

facing Trafalgar Square when the misunderstanding
—if it was a misunderstanding—happened.

According to Mallard's version they were all there
waiting for their chance to cross the double traffic
beyond the Arch, which happened that evening to
be very crowded. The light was falling. It was a
matter of choosing the right time skilfully and
dodging across when he could. He happened to
get across first, and, on reaching the other side,
walked slowly on for the others to catch him up.

According to *their* version he tried to escape.
They say that he dashed off at a most dangerous
moment when they were not thinking of crossing,
but waiting an opportunity. They were convinced
that he was bolting, and that if he did not run on
reaching the farther pavement it was only so as
not to attract attention. He certainly (they said)
walked rapidly and was all but round the corner and
lost in the crowd. This he denied. He said he had
walked quite slowly, waiting for them to cross and
catch him up.

Anyhow, whether in good faith or no, when they
had crossed they ran to come up with him and
seized him roughly upon either side. One said, so
that all could hear, " None of that ! " and gripped
his wrist and upper arm most painfully ; the other

shouted, " No you don't ! " and—so Mallard said half twisted the arm he held. Mallard broke loose. They captured him again and held him fast as the passers-by gathered round in a ring to see the fun. He struggled furiously, had nearly thrown them off when one of them produced a whistle. In a second the uniformed police had got him from them, and he was being dragged away panting, while the principal of those two original custodians, breathless, turned back his coat and showed the card of his office. It was within a hundred yards of the spot where he had suffered the same thing not three weeks before.

The rest was like a mad dream in its exact repetition. The same Police Station, the same Inspector murmuring " What, again ? " the same inscription in the same big book, the same night in the same cells, and next morning the same Stipendiary Magistrate listening with grand impartiality to the evidence.

Not till it had been given and Mr. Service had cleared his throat to give his decision did the programme change, and even then only in one particular, the verdict.

Once more did those organ tones ring out denouncing evil-doers and maintaining order in the land. But now it was the Police who were right

Repeated Impartiality of Mr. Stipendiary Service
while hearing evidence

and Richard who was wrong. The awful voice denounced in accents of implacable energy the wickedness and folly of his act. Mr. Service had heard the evidence He was fully satisfied. A more wanton and unprovoked attack he had never had to deal with in that court. He was about to pass sentence, when from the Police side Representations were made. Now such Representations are all powerful on the occasions, and there was a Remand for further proceedings. Bail ? Certainly not ! There could be no question of Bail ! The prisoner was led off, as Sarah Pickford was called, the next case, and the mighty car of justice rolled along.

And there was Richard Mallard ; lagged, as Lady Caroline Balcombe had put it ; jugged as an older fashion prefers. Pinched let us say, or, anyhow, safely in quod. What ?

Stern denunciation by Mr. Service of Mr. Richard
Mallard for interfering with the
Liberty of the Police

CHAPTER X

FROM that lonely pinnacle of rock upon the foreshore of Labrador Chap 1 did not perceive a friendly sail, a British ship all full of gallant tars. He did not catch through the telescope with which he did not sweep the horizon the blessed symbol of liberty floating at the main. Contrariwise his relief came in another fashion. A lantern flashed in his eyes under the tarpaulin tent where he lay exhausted after the tenth day of his vigil, and one of the returning party from civilisation waked him with his boot. It was not a romantic salvation ; but salvation it was, and he had seen enough of life to take it as it came.

It was about a week later that he sailed from Quebec, having first sent such cables as are despatched by people of this kind to other people of their kind (with whom London is swarming).

It was about ten days after that that he landed at Plymouth. There he was met by one of the

Red Brethren, who treated him with the deference due to superiors in that world which proposes to destroy human inequalities. The man rubbed his hands and grovelled, and Chap 1 treated him with due condescension.

In that language of theirs, which is not ours, he gave his orders.

He was not coming up to London ; he was going to a small place that had been recommended to him up-country on the edge of Dartmoor, and there he would wait till he got the news. I cannot deny the capacity of Chap 1, though I am not very fond of the type. All was worked out and simple, direct, arranged with the utmost economy. The Delegate of the Brethren, the black-bearded man who was waiting so deferentially for orders, was to go back to London and to get in touch in the way he knew. He was to propose no dealings with private firms ; he was to approach the Government direct. He had authority to offer the Concession for fifty years under an annual rental which he defined—in sterling, payable on such and such dates into the Caspian Bank in the City of London.

It was all as straightforward and rapid as buying a hat in a shop. West Irania wanted the money ; Great Britain wanted the Eremin ; and if they

Landing and Orders of Chap 1

were agreeable, he was. When the preliminaries were clinched and he was sure, he'd come up to London and end it all up properly in person—meanwhile, that was all.

The black-bearded one bowed again deferentially, and over Chap 1's face slowly spread a Mongolian smile, consonant with his Mongolian cheek-bones.

" Yes ? " he said, in the unknown tongue.

The bass of Blackbeard murmured, vibrating, in that strange language : " And what about the Rest ? " He could not believe that so great a man would strike such bargains without a commission, or at least some little financial courtesy from the Government to whom the Concession was awarded. It seemed out of nature. He was so moved by so exceedingly unbusinesslike a way of going on, that he very humbly and very dutifully protested. It had come to his knowledge, he said, that the British Government were quite willing . . . in fact, that they had already set aside quite a large Personal Recognition. He had had definite information through a gentleman who was in a position to overhear what was said when the Foreign Secretary conferred with her permanent Under-Secretary, that a counter-concession . . .

Chap 1 (his smile becoming still more Mongolian)

wagged a finger in the air, and in that same language replied.

" Brotherkin, brotherkin, to whom is the annual rental paid ? "

" To the Caspian Bank, Excellency."

" And to whose account at the Caspian Bank ? " asked the quizzing voice.

" To that of the West Iranian Government, your Excellency."

The smile faded from the Mongolian face, and the skull to which it was attached nodded like a china mandarin.

" I am the West Iranian Government," it said tonelessly.   " Be off."

*   *   *   *

It was late at night, but Caroline Balcombe was still poring over the papers before her. She had Mary Bullar at the other end of the wire. A decision had to be taken, and it was not easy.

Deep in his dungeon, remanded, the unfortunate Mallard lay. So far so good. But-that got them no forrarder, except that it prevented anyone else getting at him. Perhaps he'd be reseasonable after all.

He had always made the same reply, which had

left them exasperated. It was not heroism ; it was blank nothingness and void, that put him into this posture ; and the great statesmen—I mean states women—had to decide what they would do next.

As Caroline Balcombe considered the position, Callingham appeared.

" Do you know what's happened ? " he said.

" He's consented ? " she cried eagerly.

Callingham shook his head.

" Much more extraordinary," he said. " He can't consent to anything. Somebody else has appeared, who *can*."

" What do you mean ? " she said, confused, excited eagerly attentive.

" It wasn't him after all," said Callingham.

" *What ?* " shouted Caroline Balcombe.

Callingham enjoyed her excitement. He had spent three hours confirming and reconfirming. He had received Blackbeard direct ; he had had cross-evidence collected at once ; he had alarmed the Home Office ; he had compared the papers ; he had called in his colleagues, and all had agreed.

" The real man has turned up," he said briefly.

" How do you mean—the real man ? "

" West Irania," snapped Callingham. " He's lying *perdu* somewhere in Devon, and our old friend the

Double Cross—you know, the man who tried to blackmail the Lord Chancellor—has come from him with a very definite proposition—a very definite proposition indeed."

" Then who's Mallard ? "

" Oh, Mallard ? " said Callingham carelessly. " Mallard's Mallard. That's the great news."

" You mean—he's *really* called Mallard ? And he really *is* from Cuba ? "

" Certainly . . . And a fool," said Callingham mildly. " To-morrow morning Double Cross will be here at ten. I have made all the arrangements ; and he'll give you a memorandum of everything. We can go into the figures to-morrow. When the preliminaries are fixed and he's safeguarded he'll come up himself and settle all details and sign. It's a good offer." And he sighed with relief.

Caroline Balcombe was thinking. With the entry of her sex into public life all those years ago there had entered new forces. She was thinking of two things very important to her ; and both connected with the saving of face. One was the saving of her own face with Mary Bullar, and the other was the saving of face for all of them with the public.

If this came out ! If in his righteous indignation the innocent Mallard should talk ! . . .

"One moment, Callingham, do you know what Mallard's worth?"

"Well we've gone into that for you. Of course, we don't know to a hundred, but there's the class he travels and what he buys and his hotel. Also his clothes and his luggage . . . and now and then he wants to buy something modest and can't. Oh, I should say 1,200? 1,500 a year? Not more. He's a modest bachelor tourist . . . Poor devil!" he added, remembering with some remorse what the Modest Bachelor Tourist had gone through.

Caroline Balcombe reached out towards her books of reference and looked up the sailings. By the time she had found what she wanted she had fixed on her policy. Her mind was made up. She got Mary Bullar on the other end of the wire . . .

". . . No, don't go to bed, I've got news for you. I'm coming round at once . . . Decided? I should jolly well think I had decided! . . . Oh, you'll understand all right." And she put up the receiver as one might slam a door.

Five minutes later she had walked into the big room in Downing Street where her chief was seated at the massive writing table alone in her arm-chair, her head resting upon her hand, half asleep with

20

the long vigil.   Caroline Balcombe swept in, carefully shut the door behind her, pushed up a neighbouring chair to cover the keyhole, wagged her lorgnette at the Prime Minister, and uttered these memorable words :

"Mary, you're a chump!"

"What?" said Mary Bullar, thoroughly awake and falling backward in her chair.

"A chump, I said. A chump. You're a chump, Mary. You've got hold of the wrong man!"

"I've got hold of the wrong . . ."

"Yes," continued Caroline Balcombe, following up the surprise and throwing in her cavalry. "The Wrong Man. You've been on a wild-goose chase, all of you. I was the only one who saw it," she continued, more and more voluble. "I said so from the beginning. I had my suspicions from the beginning. I've always said he couldn't be acting. I said Mallard wasn't the man, didn't I?"

"*You* said . . ." gasped the indignant but stunned Prime Minister.

"Yes, *I* said. I said so from the beginning. I got more and more convinced. I warned you, but you wouldn't listen to me."

"Caroline Balcombe! . . ." began emphatically the contralto voice. But the soprano cut in with a torrent.

Lady Caroline Balcombe announcing to the Prime
Minister the news that the Prime Minister
is a Chump

" Yes, but you wouldn't listen to me. You never will. It's just like you ! It's you all over. *I've* had to do all the work. And now I've found out all about him—no thanks to you. The real man has turned up, and he's sent a man who's opening the negotiations to-morrow morning. Oh I've seen to it all. I've arranged everything. I've had to " (bitterly). " It's always I who have to do everything."

Mary Bullar had so far recovered that she could receive into her brain that same thought which had flashed earlier upon her colleague. Mallard must be stopped from talking. If Delisport got it into his papers . . . ! She shivered !

And another thought flashed into the fatigued but awakened brain of Mary Bullar If. Caroline followed this up Caroline would supplant her: Caroline in her turn would be Prime Minister of England. Oh, horrid thought ! For those who said that political positions had ceased to count many years ago did not allow for the effect of the women. *They* are still fairly new to the game. And they still think it great fun to be Prime Ministers, front benchers, and all the rest of it. They have added a good fifty years to the dying system.

No ; Mary Bullar didn't like the prospect at all,
She disliked being called a chump, but that was
all in the day's work. She disliked being made a
fool of ; but, after all, politicians are there for that,
and if they are going to complain, we shall have
complaints from the cocoanut shies and the clowns,
for they also are fair game. But she drew the line
at being publicly exposed in his monstrous error.

No. Mallard must be arranged. And how ?

It was Caroline Balcombe, of course, who in that
midnight hour knew what to do and did it at once.
There was a contemptuous smile on her thin lips.

" Leave it to me," she said, and she took up the
telephone.

There is a great tradition of public liberty whereby
no free man in this island may be imprisoned save
by the act of a policeman, a C.I.D. man, a nark, or
anything of that sort. But there is no rule whereby
a gentleman, once lagged, may not be released.

Indeed, I could quote you here and now, if you
had the leisure or I the time, a most amusing story
of a man who was found passing delightful days
on a beach in Normandy at the very moment
when he was officially doing time at Dartmoor for
embezzlement. Such is the beauty of an elastic
system, and to hell with all codes and kickshaws.

The streets of London at midnight are open enough. It does not take long for a prisoner to dress. And the two ladies had sat through a very brief but hostile silence when Richard Mallard appeared before them, absurdly guarded. His guardians were at once, and almost angrily, dismissed. He was greeted with a courtesy bordering on effusion. He was still half asleep and wholly wild.

"Mr. Mallard," began Mary Bullar very courteously.

"Let *me*," broke in Caroline Balcombe imperiously. "Mr. Mallard," she went on, "the Government" (how finely she pronounced that phrase!) "have had information which renders it in their eyes imperative" (oh, she could swing it, could Caroline!) "that certain steps should be taken."

Richard Mallard's heart sank. They couldn't hang him, he supposed. What were they going to do? Eh? What?

"Mr. Mallard, I will put it very briefly, and ask for your decision at once. Will you accept the sum of twelve hundred and fifty-*two* pounds a year for life" (Oh, genius of precision and detail! Her rival could not but admire!) "payable quarterly to your bank in Havana, under an agreement that shall be made out, with a copy for you to deposit in the same place?"

"Will I accept . . ." began Mallard.

"Yes," sharply interposed the Secretary of State for Foreign Affairs. "It's very simple. Yes or No? We find that you have suffered unjustly." She threw herself back. "And our experts have arrived at this figure as the compensation which is due to you. Yes or no, Mr. Mallard. And at once."

"But I don't see that I've any right, what ? . . ." began the unhappy prisoner. Caroline Balcombe shook her head impatiently.

"The alternative is that you go back and the proceedings will be continued. If you accept, we will send for your luggage ; you shall be free and in a suite reserved for you at the Cosmopolitan within an hour, and a ticket and berth reserved for you on the *Emphatic*, which sails to-morrow."

"But I thought, you know, that you said just now that it was all a mistake, what ? "

"Oh, no more of that ! " she continued savagely. "Will you or will you not ? "

"Eh, what ? Of course I will," he stammered. "You know, I don't want to go back to . . ."

She cut him short.

"Mr. Mallard," she added gravely, "there is one condition attaching to this grant, and one only. It is made freely by the Government, as I have informed **you** ; and we are happy to think that in some measure we have repaired a grave error, and that we may hope in some degree to compensate you for the, well, the *disagreeableness* you have suffered. But the condition is essential. All that has passed between you and the various negotiations for Concession must remain absolutely secret. On the day when we discover that you have made allusion to them (even in conversation)—and we are not ill-informed—not only shall the payments cease, but we will at once initiate proceedings for extradition."

" Oh, ah . . . yes, what ? " answered poor Richard.

" Do you agree ? "

" Oh, yes, I agree," he said wildly. " Eh ? "

" Very well then, Mr. Mallard. You shall leave for your hotel at once. To-morrow morning your ticket will reach you, by my own Secretary, and with it the Agreement in duplicate, and when you are once on board the first instalment shall be put into your hand."

I need not add for the intelligent reader that the sum thus provided appears on the Estimates as " Butter for the Garrison of Singapore." Though what on earth they can do with butter in a climate like that . . . However, I can't be bothered.

EPILOGUE

" EARTH can show no more majestic sight than the
Front Bench of the House of Commons. There
the highest intelligence of the nation, wedded to
its noblest characters vie one with another in the
display of eloquence and wisdom ; of foresight, of
practical ability, and of exalted virtue."

If this were true—as it was—in Huggin's time
when the 20th century was still young and women in
public life but a rarity, how much more true is it
to-day, when they occupy many among the chief
offices of State ?

Never was that Pageant more tremendous than
on the night of July 8th, 1979, some three days
after the sailing homewards of Richard Mallard
from the hospitable shores of England, and a few
hours after the last agreements upon the Eremin
Deposits of West Irania.

Mary Bullar sat in regal dignity awaiting the
moment when she should reply for herself and all
her colleagues to an indictment which was being

305

delivered with intemperate zeal upon a recent point of policy. At her side all her great colleagues sat in rank, her cousin, the dignified Sir Henry Hardham, next her, peculiarly interested in the debate, which largely concerned his Department of Home Affairs, and the rest in order beyond.

Immediately behind her the faithful and industrious Miss Wurzle, Member for Rutland, attended, to prompt if need be, and looking forward in her own mind to the day when so many years of devoted service might permit her at last to leap over the obstacle before her and take her well-earned place among the greatest in the land.

And what was the occasion of such high debate ?

It was all along of Arabella Slackett. With the sure instinct of the Born Fanatic, she had got hold of the Wrong End of the Stick and, not a member of the House itself, she had coached another Born Fanatic, who was a member, to hurl the lightning bolts of indignation at the administration of the nation. She had held out to him the Wrong End of the Stick like a sceptre of command, and the other B.F. had seized it triumphantly.

For Balmy Jane had heard three-quarters of the story and had got it top side down and twisted.

Hence the speech to which the Front Bench were listening in silent scorn.

It poured from the lips of one of the wildest of the wild men : an Annihilationist of the purest type, a man who was a Party of One, Cannock of Cardiff. His flaming red hair, his burning coals of eyes added to the effect of his lean figure, his violent gesture, his trembling wrath.

He defied the Home Office, the Foreign Office, the Prime Minister herself, to deny the facts that had come to his knowledge.

They had seized upon that great man the secret Envoy from West Irania, they had put him to every form of moral torture in their hatred of those who were liberating mankind. They had pursued him with their spies, they had driven him almost mad with their persecutions. They had thrust him and the great interests in Eremin for which he stood, and of which he was a Trustee for the Human Race, into the Lairs of Capitalists—he could name them if necessary—and when he fled over seas to avoid their infamous machinations, they had caused the miserable cowards of another Government to hand him over hand and foot to be their victim. Even now—the voice of the B.F. rose to a shriek of passion—even now he languished in a dungeon : not even brought to trial ! But Justice, though slow-footed, was sure. This exposure of which the speaker was the humble instrument would destroy the web of infamy and one more step would have been taken towards the Rising Dawn of the World.

He sat down. He did indeed.

Then did Mary Bullar rise in her majesty and with her the Ancient Might of the Constitution. She began in restrained, though powerful pose by deploring the exhibition of ill-taste—and worse—to which they had all listened. For herself, she was glad that she had a better opinion of her fellow-women than seemed compatible with the mind of the Hon. Member for Cardiff. She proceeded with more animation to denounce a condition of mind which, under the privileges of that House, could make accusations it dare not repeat outside. Her powerful contralto rose in full diapason as with outstretched arm she proclaimed outcast from the English name those who descended to practices unworthy of England ; and as the menacing forefinger of her left hand and the substantial arm which bore it extended shook with emotion they seemed to convey the full weight of Divine Vengeance against falsehood.

" These accusations," she cried, " pass from one foul

Mary Bullar, Prime Minister of England, denouncing the un-English slanders of the Wild Men

lip to another in the dark, like venomous snakes, defiling what they dare not openly engage ; their authors trust to the sly and secret action of suggestion and innuendo.   Facts they have none.   Evidence they have none.   Their sole property is rabbledabble hate of the posterity of others ! "

All sections of the House were, by this time, roused to the highest pitch of emotion.   All eyes were fixed in righteous wrath upon the wretched author of the attack which this magnificent defence had crushed.   And Miss Wurzle, as the last words rang in her adoring ears, felt that she had been witness to something more than could be due to merely human powers.   In such a moment she felt content to remain glued on to the Back Bench, to forego her hopes of office for ever, if only for the privilege of serving such towering genius.

So far Mary Bullar had spoken from an accurate memory and with deliberate inflection the words she had long prepared and learnt by heart.   She had got them all right but two.*

For a moment she paused in silence.   The air was tense.   Then in a much lower tone, even, deliberate, final, she concluded.

---

* " Rabbledabble " for " Ineradicable " and " Posterity " for " Prosperity."

"And what is the truth ? So far from his Excellency the Envoy deputed by the Republic of West Irania having passed through the Trials a disordered imagination has put before this House, he has been in this country for but a few days, which have been spent partly in visiting Devonshire, for the beauties of which county he has an affection born of old acquaintance in the past, partly at the house of my Rt. Hon. Friend the Secretary of State for Home Affairs. So far from having, as has been insanely advanced, ' languishing ' (was that the word ?) in a ' dungeon,' he was only this day a respected and honoured guest at my own table . . ."

Then came the clinch.

". . . and we brought to a fortunate conclusion the negotiations between our respective Governments, whereby the Eremin Deposits of which his country is justly proud are available to us under a generous concession for no less than thirty-five years."

The House burst into a roar of cheering, the like of which has not been heard since the conclusion of peace after the Second Asiatic War, and in the prolonged and rising roar of applause the halting apologies of the Member for Cardiff were hardly heard.

*　　　*　　　*　　　*

But Balmy Jane still holds firm to her Faith, and she will spend some years in attempting to worm out from her relations and hosts in half the country houses of England where the true, the original, Envoy of West Irania (or his murdered corpse) may lie concealed.